Triple Crown Publications Presents

RAGE TIMES FURY

Compilation and Introduction copyright © 2004 by
Triple Crown Publications
PO Box 247378
Columbus, Ohio 43219
www.TripleCrownPublications.com

Library of Congress Control Number:
2004101399
ISBN# 0-9747895-0-X
ISBN 13: 978-0-9747895-0-7
Consulting: Vickie M. Stringer

First Trade Paperback Edition Printing
February 2004

Printed in the United States of America

acknowledgments & dedications

"*I would like to Thank my family, friends and everyone who has supported me.*"

What would you do to defend or protect your family? How far are you willing to go for family? I used to ask myself these questions and I thought it was definite as to how I would react and what I would do if someone tried to harm my family. It's easy to say what you would do, how you would kill, or go all out for your family if there were a threat to them when you're at home watching at home watching the news. However, if tragedy were to occur, then it becomes real –very real. The emotions are real and the pain is real. It's an indescribable pain that no one, who hasn't experienced it, could understand. You have serious decisions to make as to how you're going to deal with it. It's not about talk any longer. I now know how far I would go for my family. As I sit in this courtroom, waiting to hear the verdict, I think of the events that brought me to this point in time and the answers to my questions.

Chapter 1

Crown Heights, Brooklyn; specifically, Crown Heights Plaza, a middle-income co-op housing development where the buildings and surrounding area are well kept and the Plaza, as we call it, has it's own Department of Public Safety. That's basically Plaza security.

The occupants are a mix of older Jewish people, and middle-aged blacks and Hispanics. It's also home to young families wanting a relatively safe place to raise their kids. It's cool here.

I was born and raised here for all of my 27 years. My name is Malik Ford. I have an apartment in the same building I grew up in. I live with my girl, Soraya, and my two sons. Malik Jr. is 5 years old and Brian is 3. I'm working hard at UPS and saving money so wifey and I can get married within a couple of years, just to make it legal and all. As she's told me before, she doesn't want to be a girlfriend forever. Damn, I love her.

I have a little "get around car." I call it that because it's just to get me around in. It's nothing extravagant, but it's sufficient. I feel I'm in a good place right now. I'm trying to maintain and build at the same time.

It was a humid July afternoon and it was beaming hot outside. I just got off from work and the dollar van was pulling up to the corner of my block to let me off. I was glad to be getting out because if it was 85 degrees outside, it had to be 90° in the van. My back and chest were wet with sweat and I was constantly peeling my shirt off my body because of it. All the windows were open but it was blowing in hot air. There were four other people on the van, which tells you how uncomfortable it was. But don't get me wrong, I'd rather pay $1 for the van and get home faster than pay $1.50 for the city bus and wait at the hot ass bus stop. The van driver is my man, Delroy, a Jamaican dude.

"Yo, Delroy," I joked. "You have to get your air conditioning fixed. You're killing us in here."

"Drive your car then," he told me in his heavy accent.

"If there were some place to park around my job, I would." I replied. Plus my air conditioner wasn't working either.

"Respect, Delroy," I said as I got off the van and handed him my dollar.

"Respect," he replied as he drove off to pack more people into his mobile sauna.

It seemed that everyone was outside that day. Little kids were running around making noise and having a good time. A bunch of kids gathered around the ice cream truck, money in hand, waiting their turn for ice cream cones and icys.

There were adults lounging on the benches in front of my building sipping on their bottled water. Parents were catching up on neighborhood issues and the latest gossip while watching their kids run around.

I saw my peoples, Chuck and Roberto, talking in front of my building. They're two of my best friends in the world. We've been cool since fourth grade.

"What's up y'all?" I said as I gave a pound to both. "What's the deal?"

"I can't call it," replied Chuck. "Your mom was out here earlier with your sons."

"Oh yeah?" I asked. Before I could say anything else, Roberto blurted out "Mack got shot!"

"What?" I asked in surprise. I heard what he said but I wanted to make sure I heard correctly.

"You heard me," Roberto continued, "Mack got shot over on Lewis Avenue, right in front of the Bravo Supermarket. He got hit four times. He ain't dead though. He's a lucky motherfucka in that respect but he's in critical condition. He may not make it."

In no way did I think that Mack being shot would have a direct effect on my life. Why would it? I'm not cool with him like that. He lives in the building next to mine. We know of each other but when we see each other on the street or wherever, we just nod our heads in acknowledgement and keep on moving. I'm cooler with his brother, Rick. Mack is one of those wild, thug motherfuckas. He likes to talk mad shit, much more so when he's drunk. He also loves to fight. He'll set it off on you quickly.

"Who did it?" I asked Roberto.

"Who do you think?" Chuck asked in a way that suggested I should already know.

Drugs was the first person that came to mind. Sean Simmons or Drugs as he's called, hustles crack and weed out of the nearby Woodson Houses. He has those projects locked down. He's the leader of a crew of about 35 to 40 people. He'll do and has done anything to protect and maintain his "business." The cops don't even mess with him too much. It's

7

rumored that he even has some on his payroll but I don't know how true that is.

We went to the same elementary school together. Drugs and I have known each other since we were eight years old. In my younger days, I used to hustle also. Drugs and I started hustling together back in the day. We used to make "runs" back and forth from Virginia chasing that easy money. Luckily, I got out of the game before I was locked up or wound up dead. Drugs on the other hand continued hustling. Actually, I'm the one who gave him his nickname. I called him Drugs because all he wanted to do was sell street pharmaceuticals. At first, we used to talk about making enough money to start a legitimate business, and then get out of the game. He became obsessed with hustling and kept on and on with it. He built his "business" up from there. He still shows me love when we see each other in the streets. He's asked me a couple of times to get back in the game with him. I told him that I couldn't go back to doing that. He asked me why and I told him point blank, my family needs me. My sons need me here with them. There's no way that I want to leave them, no way in hell.

Two days earlier, Lou, who is always hanging out with Mack, was trying to kick it to Yvette. Yvette is Drugs girlfriend. Everyone in the hood knows that. Lou definitely knew it. As it was told to me, the whole mess started when Yvette was in the projects, chillin' with her friends. Lou and Mack approached her.

"What's up Yvette?" Mack asked. "When are you going to give me some?"

"Give you some what?" Yvette asked.

"Some of that fat ass."

"Motherfucka," she said angrily. "You're buggin' the fuck out! You know who my man is!"

"Fuck your man," Lou told her. "I'll knock that punk out. He don't want none of this."

"Yeah, we'll see motherfucka," she said. "You wouldn't be talking that shit if he were here right now."

Mack then told Yvette, "You need a real man, not no bitch ass drug seller. He ain't hitting you off right. I'll eat your pussy for an hour straight. He don't know about that."

Yvette and her friends had stunned looks on their faces at that point. Lou was laughing from everything that Mack was saying. This seemed to encourage Mack to continue with the outrageous, disrespectful shit that he was saying.

"I'll lick your ass, baby," he told her. "You know that motherfucka wouldn't do that."

"Fuck you, you ain't licking anything on me," Yvette told Mack. "You can't do shit for me. Just wait till my man finds out about all this shit you're talking. Let's see if shit is funny then motherfucka."

"Fuck Drugs," Mack said.

Yvette responded, "Alright, we'll see if you talk all that bullshit when I tell him."

They went back and forth a while longer with the arguing. Finally, Yvette and her friends angrily walked away. I know Mack and Lou have a 'don't give a fuck' attitude, but what they did was way over the line.

"So today, Mack was coming out of Bravo and they wet him," Chuck told me referring to Mack getting shot. "Now they're looking for Lou. Drugs and them are gonna wet him too. Malik, they're not playing. They've been driving around all day looking for Lou. The cops have been around all day also and Drugs and them still don't care. The cops are looking to question Drugs but they haven't caught up with him yet."

The whole neighborhood knows that Drugs shot Mack. No one is going to come forward as a witness though. Drugs has the hood on lock.

"That shit is crazy," I said to Chuck and Roberto.

Just then Roberto's attention was diverted. He said, "What's up?" to Bam.

Bam and I used to be like brothers, even cooler than Drugs and I once were. We were cool until two years ago when I let him borrow $200, of my rent money, for an emergency that he had. I told him that I needed the money back the next week because that's when my rent was due. He said I would definitely get the money back before then. The day before my rent was due, I still hadn't gotten the money back. Bam acted like I was bothering him by asking for my money back. The next day, he told me he was waiting for some money. He said he was going to get it later on that day. It was from some hustle he was into, but he still gave me attitude. I extended myself because we were cool like that and him getting an attitude was fucked up. I had to borrow $200 from my mom to get my rent in on time. I was pissed. He finally gave the money back, two days later. He didn't give it to me directly though; he gave it to Soraya. We haven't spoken since that incident. I see him around with his son, who is the same age as my oldest. We don't say anything to each other though. What's ironic is even though Bam and I don't speak; our sons are cool with each other. They've known each other since birth practically. I know they want to play together more often but because of our beef, Malik Jr. doesn't go to their house and Bam's son, Darren, doesn't come to ours.

"Don't call that motherfucka over here." I said to Roberto.

Chuck said, "That beef ya'll had was from two years ago. Ya'll should squash all that. Ya'll used to be mad cool."

"Exactly, we used to be cool. We're not cool now. Fuck him." I replied.

Bam walked towards us and gave Chuck a pound. Then he gave Roberto a pound. That's where the pounds ended.

"What's up ya'll?" He asked in his deep baritone.

"I can't call it," Roberto replied.

"Coolin'," Chuck responded.

Bam and I didn't acknowledge each other and I made up my face as to say, 'Don't even bother extending your hand for a pound this way motherfucka.'

"Did you hear what happened to Mack?" Roberto asked Bam.

"Yeah," he replied. "Eric just told me."

At that point, I said, "later ya'll." I gave both Chuck and Roberto pounds. I ignored Bam and went into my building.

Chapter 2

"**M**a, it's me," I yelled loudly after ringing the bell to my mother's apartment. She answered the door and asked me, "Why didn't you use your key?"

"I didn't feel like taking it out of my pocket." I told her only half jokingly. "Hello to you too."

"Hello sweetheart," she responded as I gave her a kiss on her cheek.

"Where are the boys?" I asked.

"Soraya took them home already." She told me. "Did you know that guy that got shot?"

"A little bit but we weren't cool like that."

"Malik," my mother said in a way that I knew she was going to tell me something serious. "You have to be careful out there. There are a lot of crazy people out there doing crazy things. What happened with that guy that got shot could've happened to anyone.

15

These bastards have no regard for human life. They'll shoot you down in the street like a dog and not think twice about it. All these young boys want is fast, easy money and will do anything to get it. Poor Ms. Simmons raised Sean as best as she could and look what kind of life he chose for himself. He shames his mother by selling that garbage to people and shooting up the neighborhood like this is a shooting gallery. He's so arrogant calling himself Drugs. He's an idiot! Selling that poison; they need to put him in jail. You have to be careful. Please don't hang with those guys. I don't want anything happening to you."

She really meant what she said and I felt her concern. "I don't hang out with them and I'll be careful." I told her. "I'm always careful; just don't worry yourself about it, alright?" I tried to reassure her as best I could. Looking me dead in my eyes, she paused for a moment, then responded, "Alright."

I could tell it wasn't enough to ease her fears, but there was nothing else that I could say that would. "I'll bring the boys by tomorrow." I said, as I walked towards the front door. "I love you, Ma."

"I love you baby."

We kissed each other on the cheek and I went home to see my sons.

As soon as I opened the door to my apartment, I felt the A.C. blasting and it felt good. "Daddy!" my sons screamed. I love hearing that. "Hi Daddy!" They yelled as they ran into my arms. I gave them both hugs.

"How are ya'll doing?" I asked them. "Are ya'll behaving yourselves?"

"Yes," they replied in unison.

"I'm going to ask Mommy if ya'll been behaving," I said to them.

"No," they said in unison. "You don't have to ask Mommy," Malik Jr. told me.

"Yeah, that's what I thought," I said to them with a smile on my face. I turned my attention to Soraya. "What's up baby?" I asked her. She gave me a peck on the lips, as she was preoccupied talking on the phone. She mouthed that she was talking to her cousin, Carla. I dropped down on the couch and it felt good to just relax. It sounded like Carla had drama again, from what I overheard of Soraya's end of the conversation. I'd find out about it later. Right then, it was about my sons. The enthusiasm my kids had gave me some energy to play, even though I felt drained.

Malik Jr. or M.J., as we call him, wanted me to play 'Tekken' on the Playstation 2 with him. Brian wanted to watch his Sesame Street videotape. They were both talking to me at the same time. "Daddy, I want to play the game! Daddy, I want to watch the tape!" They repeated over and over. I just looked at them, grabbed them and started tickling them. They were both laughing and trying to run from me.

"Come here so I can tickle you," I told them as I started to chase them. They in turn, tried to tackle me to the ground. They have a lot of heart. After a while, they got back to asking me to play the video game and watch the tape.

Soraya got off the phone at that point and said, "Rodney hit Carla again." Rodney is Carla's daughter's father. "Rodney hit Carla?" M.J. asked innocently. I quickly said to him, "It was an accident. Don't ever hit any girl because it's not right and you will go to jail. You know I love ya'll and I don't want ya'll doing bad things and going to jail, alright?"

"OK Daddy," M.J. responded. I turned to Brian and asked him if he understood what I said and he nodded his head but at his age, you can't expect him to understand things like that yet. I asked him again anyway, "Brian, do you understand?" I didn't give him a chance to answer as I continued, "Don't do bad things like hitting girls because I don't want ya'll going to jail and leaving us. You don't want to be bad, you want to be good."

"OK Daddy," he said just as innocently as M.J. I planned to keep reinforcing the differences between good and bad with them as they got older and hope they took heed.

"I love ya'll this much," I said to them spreading my arms wide apart.

"I love you too Daddy." M.J. replied as he spread his arms wide also. "This much!"

As long as I live, I would never get tired of hearing that. Brian acted kind of shy to tell me he loved me. I told him, "Don't ever be shy or embarrassed to tell your family that you love them, no matter how old you get or whatever happens. I love you."

"I love you Daddy." He said shyly as he gave me a big bear hug. M.J. gave me a bear hug also. They wanted to start play fighting again. I had to cut that out quickly. "Let me talk to Mommy and we'll play later," I told them. I put the Sesame Street tape on and told M.J. that I would let him play the video game afterwards.

"Soraya, you have to watch what you say in front of the kids."

"My bad," she replied as we walked towards the kitchen. "Rodney hit Carla because they were having an argument about

Rodney coming home at 5:30 in the morning. She asked him where he was and he said he was with his man, William. She called William's house and his girlfriend said that William was sleeping right next to her. When Rodney got home, she started flipping on him. She asked him what bitch he was fucking. Then that motherfucka tried to turn the shit around by asking, 'Why the fuck is she spying on him and being paranoid." She said that they were arguing for a while and she was so mad that she threw a bottle of his cologne at him and hit him dead in the chest."

"Wow," I said. "She should have hit him in his fuckin' face," Soraya said to me. M.J. came in the kitchen at that point and asked for something to drink. I gave him two Kool-Aid Bursts so he could give one to his brother. When Brian watches Sesame Street he stays quiet and glued to that screen. "Give this juice to your brother, please," I told M.J. When he left the kitchen, Soraya continued the story. "So, she threw the cologne at his chest and he got pissed and japped her. Carla said she couldn't believe that he just hit her like that -- like it was nothing. She said she was shocked. She started throwing punches at him like crazy but he kept blocking them. He was yelling for her to calm down but she kept trying to punch him. She was screaming for him to pack his shit and get the fuck out. If he didn't, she'd throw his clothes in the street. So finally, he just left. He hasn't been back yet. She said it's over between them but she's said that before."

Soraya was right. They've had fistfights before and they've stayed together. What makes this incident any different? Carla is cool people but she needs to get out of that situation for her and her daughters' sake. "She needs to leave that situation." I told Soraya. "If there's anything she needs, she knows we'll look out for her."

"I agree," Soraya replied. "She said she might come here tomorrow or Sunday."

"Alright."

I got preoccupied because Soraya was wearing a pair of little cut off jean shorts. Her legs are shining and she was looking good. I gave her a passionate kiss and that's all it takes for me to be ready. I'm ready to bang it out. "Put the kids to bed early so we can be alone," I told her.

"OK baby," she responded. Just then, the kids came running in the kitchen. The Sesame Street tape must've ended because they came just in time to cock block. M.J. wanted to play the videogame and Brian wanted me to rewind the tape so he could watch it again.

The phone rang and Soraya answered it. "It's Chuck." She gave me the phone and left the kitchen to attend to the boys. "Yo," Chuck said, "Come to the crib. I got this new 50 Cent joint I want you to hear. They're dissin' Ja Rule on it."

"Nah, I'm chillin' with family today," I told Chuck. "I'll check it out tomorrow."

"Alright then," Chuck said. "Everything alright?"

"Yeah, I'm cool," I responded. "I'm just tired."

"I'll speak to you tomorrow then," he said.

"Later Chuck."

"Soraya," I called out. "Come here."

"What's up babe?" she asked. "Did you hear about Mack getting shot?" I asked.

"Yeah, your mom was telling me when I picked the boys up. That's messed up. Do you know if he's dead?"

"Last I heard he was in critical condition," I replied. "Rick is going to flip. I hope it doesn't get too crazy out here."

Chapter 3

The next day was Saturday and it was a relief not to be working. I just wanted to recharge and chill with the family. I was going to take the boys to the park. I love spending time with my family. I love them to death. I can't understand how some so-called fathers don't want to spend time with their kids. To me, they're pieces of shit, but I digress.

As I left my building with my sons, the first thing that caught my attention was how the front of the building was conspicuously absent of people. For a Saturday afternoon in July, there were usually a lot more people out. The Plaza security was around, but it seemed that people were still nervous to be outside with the threat of more violence looming. I could understand that. People knew what Drugs was capable of. They knew that there might be retaliation from Rick and Lou, for Mack's shooting.

You could sense the tension. Even though there weren't many people out, you could still tell that something wasn't right. As we walked on, Brian said, "Look Daddy, there's Eric."

"Shh, chill we have to go," I told him. Eric hadn't seen me yet and I didn't want him to. Eric is a local dude that could talk you to death. He always seemed to know everyone's business and he was always telling other people's business. He'd dime anyone out for any amount of money. If he were a crackhead, I could say that was the reason he snitches. The thing is, he just likes talking to hear himself talk. He likes to gossip. He's gotten his ass kicked a few times for snitching and putting peoples' business in the street.

"Yo Malik, What's up?" he asked loudly.

Damn, he saw me. Now he was going to talk me to death. "What's up, Eric?" I asked with no emotion whatsoever. "I'm taking my sons to the park right now and we're late."

"What's up ya'll?" Eric asked my sons as he gave them pounds.

I thought to myself, "Didn't this motherfucka hear what I said?" He only hears what he wants to hear. "I'm taking them to the park and they've been bugging me all day so, I'll talk to you later," I told Eric. He continued talking anyway.

"Yo, Mack is brain dead."

"Yeah?" I asked interested by this bit of information.

"Yeah," he replied. "They haven't taken him off life support yet. Rick told me this and he's pissed. Rick and Lou are gonna handle their business with Drugs."

"Chill," I said to him motioning to my sons as to not say anything too graphic in front of them. "Yeah, no problem." he replied.

"Let's go Daddy," they started saying. "Let's go Daddy!" I was glad that they were saying it so we could leave. "Alright Eric, I'm out." Then Eric said, "Alright, I'll tell you the rest later. I heard that Drugs didn't even know anything about Mack getting shot till after it happened."

"What?" I asked in surprise. I wanted to hear the rest of what he started telling me but my sons were pulling me away. "Let's go to the park Daddy," they screamed.

Walking to the park and feeling the heat, I remembered that I didn't bring any water for my sons. "We have to go to the store to get water first because I don't want you to get thirsty later," I told M.J.

"OK," he replied. Then he repeated, "Let's go to the park!" Luckily, we were at the bodega and their attention was diverted to Jay Z being played loudly out of a black Jaguar parked in front. I recognized whose car it was. It was Trip's car.

Trip is Drugs' right hand man and enforcer. His real name is Damien, but they call him Trip because he's a wild motherfucka.

Since he's so bad, they call him Satan or Triple Six --Trip for short. Drugs met him in Virginia after I stopped selling and came back to New York. Trip knows who I am, but we don't speak. I try to distance myself from dudes like Trip.

He walked out of the bodega and right past us, with that screw-face he always has, and into his car. He peeled out headed towards Woodson Projects. Ramos is the bodega's owner but everyone calls him Pop or Papa.

"What's up, Papa?" I asked.

"OK, OK," he replied abruptly.

"Everything alright?"

Pop didn't respond. He was preoccupied looking at the big mirror that lets him see what people in the back of the store are doing.

"You OK, Papa?" I asked again.

"Yeah," he responded with slightly more feeling. I guess he had a lot on his mind.

"Later," I said to him. He didn't answer me verbally. He just grunted. I kept it moving. "Daddy, let's go to the park!!" Brian demanded.

"We're going now so please relax," I responded. "You don't hear Malik bugging me do you? Just relax, we're going now." As soon as I said it, I regretted it. I don't like comparing my sons' with one another. I feel it causes unnecessary tension and competition between them. "I'm sorry Brian," I said. "I shouldn't have said that and I'm not mad at you. We're going to the park now."

We started off the short distance to the park and walking towards us was Ms. Riviera. Ms. Riviera is a nice older woman from the neighborhood. She's always friendly and quick with a smile, but not that day. She walked like she was in a big hurry. By the look on her face, it looked like there was something heavy on her mind.

"How are you doing, Ms. Riviera?" I asked.

"I'm alright Malik, how are you? Hi boys, you're getting big." She said as though she were obliged to do so. She kept in stride as she talked and said, "Be safe," as she kept it moving. It seemed like this recent violent episode had a lot of people on edge. That was not the first shooting in the neighborhood. There have been others, but this one seemed different. It's as if people in the hood were expecting and preparing themselves for more violence.

We finally arrived at the park and it wasn't as crowded as it usually was either. M.J. ran straight to the swings and Brian to the slide. They were close enough together that I could watch both of them. It was also close to the basketball courts. Some people I know were playing ball and some young dudes were by the bleachers shooting dice. Some teenagers were talking shit, primarily about Mack's shooting. One teen said that Drugs was not going to stop until he got Lou.

"Lou is finished. It's a wrap for him," he said. Ray, a worker for Drugs was also there.

He said, "That whole situation is not how ya'll think it is."

"What the fuck are you talking about?" the first teen asked.

"Just trust me," Ray said with emphasis. "It's not how ya'll think. I ain't going to get into specifics, but trust me."

"Cut the spy shit and say what you know," the first teen said.

"Who the fuck do you think you're talking to?" Ray fumed. "Motherfucka, if I wanted to tell you then I would have. What are you a fuckin' cop now? Don't fuckin' question me or talk to me like that. Just roll the fuckin' dice."

"Chill, Ray," another guy there told Ray. "Let it go, he didn't mean it like that. Let's just play dice."

"What's wrong Daddy?" M.J. asked after hearing the commotion on the courts.

"They're just having a little argument," I told him. "It's OK, keep playing."

"Look at me Daddy!" Brian yelled while going down the slide.

"Look Daddy," M.J. said following right behind his brother on the slide.

"That's nice ya'll," I said. "Slide down again."

"OK Daddy, look!" demanded M.J.

"That's a good slide, M.J." Just then my cell phone rang.

"Yo, Malik, guess what?" Chuck asked me as I answered it. "They jumped Rick by the train station."

"What?" I asked surprised that something would be done this soon after Mack got shot.

"They got him coming off the train. He got fucked up. I'm here at the train station right now. I didn't see him get fucked up though. I got here when the cops and the ambulance were already here. I was talking to some guys here and they were telling me what happened. They said they heard cars screeching and when they turned around, they saw about eight dudes jump out of two cars. Before Rick could react, they stomped him."

"Did they see who it was who jumped him?" I asked.

"They didn't say," Chuck replied. "I saw him when they were putting him in the ambulance though and he was opened up. It looked like he had teeth missing. There was blood all over. I don't know if he's dead though. He definitely wasn't conscious. The cops weren't letting people get too close. Drugs and them are not playing."

Chuck was right. Drugs wasn't playing but Rick had nothing to do with it. Drugs had Rick fucked up so that he wouldn't retaliate for shooting his brother. Even with the increased police presence in the area because of Mack's shooting, Drugs and them still went after Rick. Everyone knew Lou was next and everyone was bracing themselves for whatever was going to happen.

Chapter 4

We were on our way back from the park after a few hours and the heat had taken its toll on me. I was tired and wanted to get home and enjoy the A.C. M.J. and Brian still had energy, but I knew that they were going to sleep well that night. Walking back home, I thought about all that had gone on in the past few days and wondered what else had happened today, if anything. "Stay close to me," I said to M.J. and Brian. Judging from recent events, anything could've jumped off. I got on my cell and called Chuck.

"Chuck, what's up?"

"Chillin'," he replied.

"Anything new happened?" I asked.

"I haven't heard anything new since I spoke with you last. Where are you?"

"I'm coming back around the way now," I told him. "I'll be at the building in about five minutes, but I'm dropping my sons' to my moms' house."

"Alright," he said. "I'm going to come down and let you hear this 50 Cent joint, it's sick. Don't go upstairs right away, wait for me." I reluctantly agreed and we hung up.

"Are ya'll alright?" I asked M.J. and Brian.

"Yes," Brian answered kind of angrily. M.J. just nodded his head. They were upset that we left the park. If it were up to them, they'd be there from dusk till dawn.

A Lexus IS300 drove by blasting the latest Nas joint. It was Yvette and her girlfriends. While I looked at them driving by, apparently chillin', I wondered to myself whether all this drama going on was having any effect on her. Did she intend for it to go as far as it had? Did she want it to stop? Did she care if it stopped? Mack was brain dead and his brother Rick was in critical condition. This was not a game. These were real people, with real lives. Are we this desensitized to violence and peoples' lives that the events of the past few days would mean nothing to someone who is a main part of all the drama?

I've known Yvette for a long time. She's not from Crown Heights Plaza or Woodson Projects. She lives in a private house about a mile away from here. She went to a Catholic school, from elementary to high school. Ever since I've known her, she's been hanging around our way. All her boyfriends have been from around the way. She seems to like the excitement that the neighborhood gives off. She's a very materialistic person. She judge's people by the clothes they wear, car they drive or amount of money they have. It's no wonder she's with Drugs now. Yvette is a cute brown skinned girl with dimples and the kind of body that makes grown men want to do anything to please her and get on her good side. Guys would do anything to make her happy. Speaking of which, she has Drugs whipped and wrapped around her manicured fingers.

I was back around the way and I had already dropped my sons off to my mother's house. I was in front of my building waiting for Chuck. "Where was Eric?" I thought to myself. The one time I wanted to speak to this jerk and he wasn't around. He must've been somewhere getting in someone's business. I saw Roberto walking out of the building and we nodded our heads at each other as to say, What's up?' POP, POP, POP, POP, POP, POP pierced the summer afternoon. It was the unmistakable sounds of gunshots. "Oh shit!" I exclaimed as I ducked my head after hearing the first shot. I had no idea where they were coming from but judging by the recent violence, I wasn't taking any chances. They sounded like they were real close though, too close for my comfort. I looked at Roberto to see if he was OK. When the shots were first fired, he ducked down also. He was OK.

"Did you see where the bullets came from?" Roberto asked.

"Nah," I responded.

We looked up the block and saw a bunch of people running. We don't know if they were running to or from where the shots came from. The Plaza security, with sirens blaring, raced past us to the scene of the latest drama.

"C'mon Malik, let's go check it out," Roberto said. Curiosity had gotten the better of me at that point. "Yeah, let's go," I said as we headed towards the scene. "Move back, back it up!" the police officers demanded of the steadily increasing crowd of people happening around the shooting area.

That's Drugs truck," said Roberto.

"It damn sure is," I responded looking at the metallic silver Navigator with bullet holes in it. We were facing the passenger side of the truck and we could see the front of the truck had run up on the sidewalk. The right front tire was shot out. The driver and passenger side doors were both open. We heard the crowd buzzing that someone was slumped over in the back seat. Now people were trying to get a look to see if there was indeed anyone back there.

"I wonder who's in the back seat?" I asked Roberto.

"I don't know," he replied. "But it's more than likely not Drugs. He wouldn't be in the back seat of his own truck. You know he doesn't let anyone drive his shit."

"True," I responded. Then we heard someone towards the front of the crowd say, "Oh shit, it's Ray." The crowd started buzzing again. "You heard that?" I asked Roberto

"Yeah," he replied. "This shit is fuckin' crazy! Drugs left his truck? And if that is Ray, he ain't moving. It doesn't look good."

"I know," I told him. "I just saw Ray earlier today in the park. He was talking some shit about people not knowing the whole story about all this drama with Mack and Drugs."

"Yeah?" he asked.

"Yeah."

Roberto and I couldn't actually see anybody or anything in the back of the truck so I said to him, "Let's bounce. We can't see shit and I was supposed to meet Chuck in front of the building. We'll find out what happened later anyway."

"Alright," he said and then we walked off to meet Chuck.

Back around the way, Chuck was already sitting on the benches listening to his CD player. We told him where we just came from, and that we heard it may be Ray who got shot. Chuck was buggin'.

"Damn," he said. "Lou isn't playing. You knew he wasn't going to just hide. Have you seen him?"

"Nah," I replied,

"I haven't seen him either," Roberto said. "But I doubt he's staying around here. He's not stupid. Well, not that stupid."

"Let me hear that 50 Cent joint," I told Chuck. I was mad tired at that point and I wanted to go upstairs and chill. I bopped my head to the beat of the music, but I was not really listening to the lyrics because when I listen to something for the first time, I always listen to the beat first. Anyway, I'd been out all day and I needed some rest. "This shit is hot," I told Chuck. "They're dissin' the shit out of Ja Rule." I said to Chuck knowing damn well I didn't listen to the lyrics. I handed him back the CD player and said, "I'm going upstairs. Let me know if you find anything out."

"Alright, later" they responded. I was finally going to be able to get some rest, or so I thought.

I walked into my house and heard Soraya talking. Then I heard another voice. I went into the living room and it was Carla. Damn, there goes my rest. "What's up Carla?" I asked.

"I'm alright."

"What's up baby?" I asked Soraya as I gave her a kiss.

"I'm good," she answered. "Carla was just telling me the latest."

"Which is?" I asked.

"Rodney came home this morning and we were arguing again," Carla explained. "He came in acting like nothing was wrong which pissed me off more. He thought it was a joke until he walked in the bedroom and saw his clothes were packed. He asked what the fuck I was doing packing his shit and said he wasn't leaving. So we were arguing for a while and I told him when I came back, I wanted him and all his shit out."

"You're serious this time?" I asked her.

"Hell yeah!" she said. "It's over this time for good."

"Where was your daughter during all this?" I asked.

"Kari was with my mother. She's been there all week."

"Luckily," I said to her. Then Soraya told me, "Carla's spending the night. She doesn't

43

want to go home and deal with him if he's still there."

"What if he's still there tomorrow?" I asked. "Then I'm going to call the cops," she responded. "I'm not dealing with that anymore."

"OK," I said. "I hope you stick to it this time because you and Kari shouldn't be exposed to that."

"I know we shouldn't," she said. "And I'm not going to put up with it anymore. I'm tired of that shit."

The doorbell rang and from outside the door I heard M.J. and Brian yelling, "Daddy, open the door Daddy!" I opened the door and they rushed in and gave me a hug. "What's up Daddy?" M.J. asked.

"I'm chillin'," I told him.

"We missed you," M.J. added. "Yeah, we missed you," Brian told me.

"I missed ya'll too. Did ya'll behave yourselves?"

"Yes," they told me.

"Did they?" I asked my mother.

"Yeah, they were OK," she said in a tone that implied that they acted up a bit. "Hi Mommy, hi Auntie Carla," the boys screamed. My mom said hello to everyone and sat in the living room. Soraya started to tell Carla the latest about what was going on around the way. With my mom there, I knew all three of them were going to be talking for a long time. I didn't want M.J. and Brian to hear what they would be talking about. "C'mon, let's go play in the back," I told the boys. "Daddy, let's go to the park please," Brian requested.

"It's too late to go now," I told him.

"Can we go tomorrow?" he then asked.

"When I wake up, I'll take you."

"OK," they said excitedly. I knew they were going to wake me up real early. I needed to get some rest but that was not going to happen at this time. My boys wanted to play so we played. I can't front on them. "Alright," I said. "I'll take ya'll to the park tomorrow. Just let Daddy get some rest now." Of course, I played with them some more. We played until about 9 or 9:30 p.m. and it was time for them to go to bed. My mom had gone home and Carla was watching TV in the living room.

Finally, there were no more distractions. I was falling out. It was only 11:00 p.m., on a Saturday night, and I was about to go to sleep. It didn't sound exciting but fuck it, I have a family I love and I'd rather chill with them. I had to get some sleep.

Chapter 5

"Wake up Daddy! Wake up Daddy! Let's go to the park now!" I heard my sons scream. At first, I thought I was dreaming. "Daddy, get up! Let's go to the park!" they continued. They started shaking me as well as yelling for me to wake up. I began to realize it wasn't a dream. Brian was more adamant in trying to wake me up. "Let's go Daddy!" Brian demanded. It was only 9:42 a.m., on my day off from work and I was still feeling exhausted.

"Not now," I told them with weariness in my voice. "Daddy's still tired." Both of them continued to try to get me to take them to the park. "Mommy's calling ya'll," I said trying to get them to go to the kitchen to let me continue sleeping. "No she's not," M.J. replied. "Get up."

I smelled pancakes so I knew Soraya was cooking. "Where's Aunt Carla?" I asked more agitated. "She's talking to Mommy," M.J. answered. "Go ask Aunt Carla to take you to the park," I said. "No!" Brian answered defiantly. "We want to go with you. Let's go!" M.J. said.

I wanted to take them, but not that early. "Go ask Aunt Carla to take you outside and I'm going to get dressed and take ya'll to the park." I said to them.

"OK," they answered with excitement as they ran off to ask Carla.

The room was quiet again and I dozed off. "Malik, are you hungry?" Soraya asked, waking me up again. "No thanks," I replied. "Where are the boys?"

"They're in front of the building waiting for you."

I looked at the clock and it had been a half hour since the boys first tried to wake me up. "I'll eat when I come back from the park." I told Soraya. I hurriedly washed up, brushed my teeth and put on my clothes. I grabbed my keys and as I went towards the front door, Soraya told me, "Be safe baby."

I found it strange that she would say that only because she never said that to me before. "OK, I will," I answered with confusion clearly evident in my voice.

I walked out the door and pushed the elevator button. I waited there joined with the smell of one of my neighbors cooking fish. The smell was so strong that if I had stayed there any longer, that fish smell would've been imbedded in my clothes all day. Luckily, the elevator came soon after. As I got on and the door closed, I pushed the button for the first floor. I smelled my shirt. "Shit," I said to myself. Now I would have to go all day smelling like Bacalao.

What followed was something I've replayed over and over in my head and will never forget. As I walked out the front door of my building, I saw Carla sitting on the benches talking on her cell phone. M.J. and Brian were running around close to her. It seemed like everything was moving in slow motion. M.J. and Brian didn't see me at first. I walked towards them to surprise them. I don't know what made me look but I turned my head to the right and saw Lou walking in my direction. I was going to talk to him to see what was up with the whole Drugs situation. He was still walking towards me but he hadn't seen me because he was looking off to his right. I followed his eyes and he was looking at a car driving slowly in the street. I looked at Lou again and he was still looking at the car. He stopped walking for about five seconds, still staring at the car. Then he suddenly jetted towards my building. I looked back at the car and two teenagers, about 16 years old, jumped out with guns in their hands. "M.J., Brian, get down!" I yelled at the top of my lungs. The shorter teen started shooting first. The other teen shot in our direction. When I yelled for M.J. and Brian to get down, Carla saw what was happening and ran to get the boys, as she was closer to them. While I ran towards the kids, I heard more shots being fired. There were at least ten shots let off. The one shot that I do remember is the one that tore into the stomach of my oldest son!

I saw Malik Jr. get shot. At that moment, I was oblivious to anything else going on. It was like the world got silent. No, it was more like there were sounds, but they seemed like they were far away. I was only about ten feet away from the boys when M.J. was shot, but it felt like I was ten miles away. I couldn't get to my son in time. My mouth was dry and I found it hard to breathe. My heart was beating so hard it felt like it was going to burst right out of my chest. I remember thinking that this wasn't happening. It must've been a bad dream, the worst of nightmares. Carla was screaming. Her screams were such that it would pierce your soul. I could feel it in my bones. The look on her face was indescribable. It was like someone pulled her heart out. As far as I knew, they were still shooting at Lou. I was so focused on M.J.; it was as if nothing else existed in the world at that time. I finally made my way to M.J. and what I saw close up crushed me. There was blood gushing out of his wound. I had a little towel with me that I was going to use to wipe off my sweat. I used it to apply pressure to his wound. He let out a scream that made my whole body chill. I tried to relax him so he didn't go into shock. "It's OK, M.J. You'll be alright," I tried to reassure him. "Don't be scared. Daddy's here and I'm going to take care of you." Brian had been screaming and panicking since M.J. was hit. I saw that Brian wasn't shot and that relieved me. It wasn't good for M.J. to see Brian panicking. "Calm down, Brian," I told him. "He'll be alright but you have to stop screaming or you'll scare him." But he continued screaming. I told Carla to call 911 and take Brian upstairs, which she did.

M.J. was moaning in pain, his body writhing in agony on the hot concrete. I don't wish any parent the anguish of seeing their child in pain. I looked at my son losing his life with the blood leaving his body, and I was helpless. At that moment, I couldn't do anything but try and comfort him. I couldn't take the gunshot away. I couldn't take his pain away. I've never felt that helpless in my life. I've always vowed to take care and watch out for my kids. But there I was unable to take the pain away. I felt a devastating pain. I guess the shooting was over at that time because people were gathering around M.J. and I. They were talking to me but I couldn't hear what they were saying. For all I knew, they could have been speaking another language. My heart was pumping faster than before. "Are you alright?" I asked M.J. "Talk to me! Talk to Daddy!"

Soraya flew out of the building, tears pouring down her face. "Oh my God!" Soraya repeated over and over again. "Stop it, you're making him nervous," I told her. "Please don't let my baby die," she started saying. "It hurts Daddy. Please make it stop hurting," M.J. said to me right then. That crushed me. "It hurts Daddy," he repeated. "Am I going to die?"

"You're not going to die," I replied. "You're going to be alright." The towel that I had pressed against his wound was saturated with blood. The sounds of sirens were getting closer. I didn't know if it was the cops or ambulance. I didn't want to take any chances so I said, "Soraya, call the ambulance again please!" I said it as calm as I could. It took all my strength not to break down in front of M.J.

The ambulance finally arrived in what seemed like hours. Malik Jr. was still conscious. The paramedics were attending to him. "Is he going to be alright?" I asked them. I knew that they probably couldn't answer that question at that time but I needed some sort of confirmation that he would be OK.

"We're doing our best to help him," one of them answered.

"I'm riding in the ambulance with him," I said. "Let's go Soraya." Soraya was crying uncontrollably and she leaned on me as we walked towards the ambulance. "It's going to be OK," I kept telling her. We followed the stretcher with our son on it. I looked back and saw the puddle of blood, my sons' blood, and shook my head. We were in the ambulance and I held his little hand in mine. "Squeeze my hand, please," I begged him. I bent down and whispered in his ear, "Mommy and Daddy love you very much." I don't think he comprehended. He opened and closed his eyes and moaned again. The whole situation just overwhelmed me at that point and I broke down. I cried uncontrollably as Soraya held me.

We were at the hospital and I told Soraya, "He'll be alright." But I was trying to convince myself as much as I was trying to convince her. "He'd better be OK," she said to me. "I don't know what I would do without him. Who shot him?"

"Two teenagers. I didn't recognize them. They were trying to shoot Lou."

"I'm gonna fuckin' kill Drugs!" she exclaimed. "That motherfucka is dead."

"Calm down," I told her.

I couldn't even think about revenge at that time, as I was too worried about M.J. dying. I had so many things running around my head that I couldn't think clearly. As I sat there next to Soraya, with my head in my hands, I kept thinking the same things to myself. I kept thinking that this was not happening. Why couldn't I be shot instead of him? I would have gladly taken his place. "We have to call my mom and Brian," I said to Soraya.

"Please do it," she responded. "I can't do it. I can't speak to anyone now."

I understood. I tried to keep her calm. I didn't look forward to telling people about all that had happened. I didn't want to talk about it but one of us had to. I called my mom first and she was almost to the point of panic but tried to hold it in as not to make me nervous or feel worse.

"How is he?" she asked in a hushed tone.

"M.J. is still in the operating room," I said to her.

"What did the doctor say?"

"I haven't heard anything more yet," I replied. "We're still waiting to speak to him."

"How did it happen?"

I went through the whole story again. By talking about it again, all the different emotions rushed back. When I spoke on it, it felt like someone punched me through my chest and grabbed my heart out. I've never been that scared in my life.

"How are you and Soraya holding up?" she asked.

"O.K. under the circumstances," I responded. "Please pick Brian up from my house. Carla is watching him."

"How is he doing?" she asked.

"I'm going to call him now and find out." I responded. "I'll call you back when I find something out. I love you."

"I love you too and I'm going to pray for him," she said.

I hung up from her and called my house. Carla answered on the first ring. "Hello."

"Yeah Carla, it's me."

"How is he?" She asked sounding like she was bracing herself for the worst.

"He's still in the operating room. We haven't heard anything more yet."

"Where's Soraya?"

"She's in the waiting area," I responded. "She doesn't want to speak to anyone. She's real fucked up right now."

"I am so sorry," Carla said to me. "Everything happened so fast."

I cut her off by saying, "It's not your fault. You couldn't help what happened. You didn't pull the trigger. You didn't shoot him. Don't beat yourself up about it. Just pray for him and hope he turns out alright."

"I am so sorry," she said again.

"It's not your fault," I said more firmly. "My mother is going to pick Brian up and bring him to her house. How is he?"

"He's calmer now," she said. "He's sitting on the couch watching TV. He was real bad earlier, saying things like 'they killed his brother.' He was crying a lot and asking for you and Soraya. I finally calmed him down. He's not really watching anything; he's just looking at the T.V."

"Let me speak to him," I told her. I heard her say in the background, "It's Daddy, he wants to speak to you." Then I heard in a fragile voice, "Hi Daddy. Is my brother dead?"

"No Brian," I responded. "M.J. is not dead. The doctors are working right now to make him better. When I find out something more, I'll call you, OK?"

"OK," he said with sadness in his voice.

"Grandma is going to pick you up," I continued. "I need you to take care of her, alright?"

"OK," he responded. "Where's Mommy?"

"She's waiting to talk to the doctor to see if M.J. is alright," I replied. "She's going to call you later."

"Why did they try to kill M.J.?" he asked.

"Those were bad men who shot M.J., but they weren't trying to shoot him. They were shooting at someone else and M.J. was shot accidentally. That doesn't make it right. They were wrong for what they did. Those were bad people and they're going to go to jail. They didn't mean to shoot M.J."

It's hard explaining the senselessness of violence to a 3 year old and having him understand.

"Do you understand?" I asked him.

"Yes," he said but I sensed he really didn't.

"Let me speak to Auntie Carla please. I love you and I'll call you later."

"I love you Daddy," he said softly.

"Don't hang up Brian," I told him. "Put Aunt Carla on the phone."

"Auntie Carla, my Daddy wants to speak to you."

"Hello," Carla said.

"Carla, are you going to stay there or go back to your house?" I asked.

"I'm going to stay here for a while."

"Alright, I'll call you when I know something," I told her. "We can't have our cell phones on in the hospital so we'll call when we know something

--later."

"Bye."

There was despair in both of our voices as we hung up. As I walked back to the waiting area, I hoped that there would be news to report. At the same time I prepared for the worst.

Chapter 6

"What's taking them so long?" I asked Soraya rhetorically. "Someone should've come out and told us something already. This shit is fucking ridiculous. I'm going to ask the nurse if she can find something out." I walked over to the nurses' station and Nurse Moran looked up at me.

"Yes?" she asked me.

"Can you please find out about my son who was shot?" I asked her. "His name is Malik Ford Jr. We've been here for hours and no one has come to give us any news yet. Can you please find out something for us?" I guess she sensed the desperation in my voice and in my face.

"Alright, I'll find out. Give me five minutes," she replied.

"Thank you."

"What did she say?" Soraya asked as soon as I walked back to her. "She's going to find something out in five minutes."

Soraya and I held hands and quietly waited. Those five minutes we waited seemed like five hours. There were so many thoughts going through our minds. I didn't want to think about all the different things that the doctor could have told me but I couldn't help but to think about it. I squeezed Soraya's' hand harder.

"It's been six minutes. Where is she?" I asked Soraya.

"Go back and find out," she said. I went back to the nurses' station and she wasn't there. She must've still been finding out for us. I guess it was a couple of more minutes I waited there before Nurse Moran walked through the metal doors. My heart started pumping faster as I awaited the news.

"The doctor will be right out to talk to you," she told me.

"How is he?" I asked her.

"He'll explain everything to you when he comes out. He'll be right out."

"Shit," I said to myself. "Alright, thanks," I told her. I was glad that she spoke with the doctor but I wanted to now how M.J. was. I didn't want to wait any longer. Soraya walked over to me and asked," What did you find out?"

"She said the doctor is going to come out now and talk to us. She didn't tell me anything about M.J." She kissed her teeth right in front of the nurse.

"Chill," I told her. "At least she got the doctor to come talk to us finally."

We heard the metal doors open and we whipped our heads in that direction to see who was coming through them. It was a doctor walking in our direction. It seemed like he was moving in slow motion. He looked at Nurse Moran and she motioned to us.

"Hello, I'm Doctor Patel," he said. "Malik is in stable condition right now. His injuries are very serious. The next 24 to 48 hours he'll be monitored closely but he should make it."

"Thank God!" Soraya said. A sense of relief rushed over me. Soraya was relieved also as was evident by the look on her face. Dr. Patel went into the specifics of the injury but at that point I didn't pay attention. All I heard was that M.J. should make it.

"When can we see him?" Soraya asked.

"When he's moved to his room you can see him," he replied.

"Do you know how long that will be?"

"The nurse will let you know," he responded.

"Thank you," I told him with a hint of frustration.

As he walked off I told Soraya, "I'm going outside to use my cell and check the messages."

"I'm going to call your mom and Brian on the pay phone," she told me.

"Alright, I'll be back," I responded as the elevator door closed. It was 11:50 at night and as I walked through the automatic opening doors, the first thing I noticed was how cool it was outside. I turned on my phone and I had 10 voicemail messages. I started going through them.

"Malik, it's Chuck. Call me as soon as you get this message." That was the first message Chuck left me. He left me three others and Roberto left two. My mom left a couple and the rest were from some other friends. Since Soraya was going to call my mother, I was going to call the other people back. But before I forgot, I called my job and left a voicemail message explaining everything and that I wasn't coming in tomorrow. I'd call again in the morning and speak to my supervisor and let him know that I would need a few days off.

Then I called Chuck back. It was late so I called him on his cell.

"Hello," he answered groggily.

"Chuck, it's me," I told him with weariness in my voice.

"How's M.J.?"

"He's in serious but stable condition," I told him. "The doctor said that M.J. has to be closely monitored for the next 48 hours."

"Have you seen him yet?"

"Nah. We're waiting to see him now." I responded.

"How's Soraya?"

"She's alright under the circumstances."

"I went to your moms' house and was speaking to her for a while," Chuck said. "I'm glad Brian is alright."

"Yeah," I said. "We're lucky for that."

"What color was the car that those motherfuckas was driving?"

"It was a burgundy Honda Accord," I replied.

"They found it across the street from Woodson." Chuck told me. "It was a stolen car. Last I heard they hadn't caught the guys who did it yet. Did you see their faces?"

"I saw them but I didn't recognize them. It was two young dudes, like 16 or 17 years old. I didn't see the driver. But I remember those two motherfuckas faces. I'll never forget their faces." My feelings turned to anger at that point.

"What do you want to do about Drugs?" Chuck asked. "Whatever you want to do, I got your back. Fuck that, you can't let this shit slide. That motherfucka could've killed your son. That shit was fuckin' reckless. I spoke to Roberto and them and they're ready for whatever. It's on you. What's up?"

"Good lookin' out," I told Chuck. "Believe me, I'm not letting this shit slide. I'm going to fuck him up. Get all the fellas ready cause right now I don't give a fuck. This motherfucka almost killed my seed. I know I'm going to want to shoot Drugs once I see M.J. in his hospital bed. We're gonna get him. Has anyone seen that motherfucka?"

"Not yet," Chuck responded. "But I got the fellas out there getting information. Do you think that Drugs thinks that you're going to go after him for shooting M.J.?"

"I don't care what he thinks." I replied.

"That motherfucka knows how I can get down. I don't give a fuck."

"The reason I ask is if he thinks that you're going to do something to him, he may try and get you first." Chuck explained. "Just like what they did to Rick. But don't stress it. Whenever you're ready, we're gonna come pick you up from the hospital and we gonna watch your back. They're not going to snuff you like they did to Rick."

"Alright, good lookin' out," I responded. "But make sure all the fellas get as much information as possible."

"No problem, I got you," Chuck replied.

"I gotta call Roberto back," I said to Chuck. "You think he's still outside?"

"Hold on, I'll check," he said. Chuck lives in an apartment that faces the front of the building and he only lives on the 2nd floor.

"I don't see him out there. But I spoke to him earlier and don't worry, shit is in motion."

"You working tomorrow?"

"No," he responded. "I told you we're gonna pick you and Soraya up and watch your back."

"Cool," I told him. "I'm about to go back inside and see M.J. My phone's going to be off because they don't want cells on inside the hospital. So I'm going to call you when I'm ready."

"No problem, I'll have my cell on," Chuck replied.

"Stay up."

"Alright Chuck." We hung up and I prepared myself to see M.J. I got off on the floor we were previously on and Soraya was standing in the middle of the hallway.

"M.J. is on another floor now." We pushed the button to the elevator and got on.

"What floor?" I asked her.

"Fifth floor, room 505."

"You spoke to Brian?" I asked.

"Yes. He asked how M.J. was and he asked if the police caught the people who shot M.J. He also asked when we were coming

71

home. He didn't want me to get off the phone but I ran out of change. I told him to go back to sleep and we would call him tomorrow. Your mom is not going to work tomorrow. She's going to watch Brian instead of taking him to the babysitter. She said she wouldn't be able to concentrate at work and she said that she wants to come see M.J. I told her to get some sleep and we would call her tomorrow. She was relieved when I told her what the doctor said. She said the same thing as the doctor about M.J. having to be closely watched for 24 to 48 hours. She said that she's coming to see M.J. tomorrow."

"What else?" I asked.

"That was it with her," she replied. "I spoke to Carla also and told her everything. She was blaming herself for what happened to M.J."

"I know," I said. "That's what she was saying to me when I spoke to her. I told her it wasn't her fault. She didn't put M.J. here in the hospital."

"That's what I told her also. She was crying and saying that a lot of negative shit was happening around her lately. She was talking crazy. I had to calm her down. I told her it wasn't her fault and that we would talk more later on. I wasn't in the mood to hear all of that. I was trying to rush and get back here to see M.J."

At that point we were on the fifth floor walking towards room 505. Soraya continued, "Carla's going to work in the morning, so I told her to lock up and take the keys to your moms'. She said that she was going to try and see M.J. after she comes from work."

We were finally at room 505 and all the talking stopped. We walked in the room and my heart dropped. M.J. had tubes all in him. They were in his nose to help him breathe. They were in his arms. We looked at him and tears flooded our eyes. I had a rush of emotions. When I first saw M.J. in that hospital bed, I thought about how close we came to losing him. Or should I say how close it came to those two motherfuckas taking his life. I felt an incredible sadness and helplessness. No parent should ever outlive his or her children.

Then as I continued looking at M.J., my feelings changed to a tremendous anger. I felt like if anyone were to say anything to me, I would flip on them. I didn't give a fuck about anything at that point except M.J. Soraya looked at me and since she knows me so well, she knew I was mad. But the anger I felt was so strong that it was clouding my better judgment. I knew it was clouding my judgment but I didn't care. I was consumed by rage and it was directed towards Drugs.

I couldn't wait to hear some news from Chuck and them. But even more than that I couldn't wait to get back around the way to confront Drugs. I wanted to blast him. I wanted to end his life and I knew I would have no problem doing it. Messing with someone's family is something that you don't do, period. That's a line that should never be crossed.

Right then, M.J. moved and my focus switched back to him. He had been sleeping and now he began to wake up.

"Hi baby," Soraya said to him. "Mommy and daddy's here." He looked at us but didn't speak. He acknowledged us by the way he looked at us. He seemed happy to see us there. I'm glad we were the first faces he saw when he did open his eyes. But he closed his eyes again and Soraya and I looked at the monitor. It was OK, no flat line so he must've went back to sleep. It must've been the medication that made him groggy.

"I want to see his scar," I said to Soraya.

"Go ahead," she responded. I gently pulled up his gown.

"Be careful." A bandage covered the scar and I felt a surge of anger again. I slumped down in one of the chairs in the room and I just stared at M.J. I extended my hand to Soraya to come sit next to me. But she chose to sit on the other side of the bed, next to M.J., and hold his hand. While she was holding his hand in hers, she put them to her head and prayed. I stared at M.J. to see if there was any movement from him. I found myself nodding off. I was exhausted. I took a few deep breaths and after a few moments, I fell out.

Chapter 7

I kept dozing on and off through the remainder of the night. It was an uncomfortable sleep that did little to relieve my fatigue. I stayed in a light sleep so that I could be aware of any movement from M.J. Soraya looked like she had an uncomfortable rest also. It was a little after 7 a.m. and I was starved. I didn't even remember the last time that I ate. All that I was doing was drinking water and my stomach was growling. As soon as I moved, Soraya woke up from her light sleep.

"I'm gonna get something from the vending machine," I told Soraya. "You want something?"

"Get me a bag of Doritos or Cheez Doodles please," she replied. "And something to drink. Orange juice or whatever they have."

I went down to the 4th floor with my breath stinking and stomach growling. When I got to the cafeteria, I saw Dr. Patel eating at one of the tables. So I walked right over to him.

"Do you remember me? I'm Malik Ford. My son was shot in his stomach."

"Yes," he said in acknowledgment.

"How is he?" I asked. "We've been with him for hours, but he's only opened his eyes once."

Dr. Patel responded by saying, "Surgery took a lot out of him. He needs a lot of rest. He's still under observation like I said before but he should be alright barring any unforeseeable complications."

To me it sounded like he was reading from a script. It seemed like he had said that hundreds of times before. I did appreciate that he took the time to talk to me. He could have been short and rude to me for interrupting him while he was having his meal. I talked all in his face with my bad breath but he was polite and reassuring in his words and tone of voice. It gave me a burst of energy and hope to counteract the rage that boiled inside of me.

I got the little bullshit snacks from the vending machine and couldn't wait to tell Soraya about the conversation I had with Dr. Patel. A nurse walked out of M.J.'s room. I walked in the door and was relieved by what I saw. M.J. was awake and talking to Soraya.

"What's up M.J.?" I asked.

"Hi Daddy," he responded barely audibly. Tears filled my eyes as I took hold of his hand.

"You're going to be alright," I told him. "I just spoke to the doctor and that's what he told me."

"OK," he said softly.

"The nurse changed his bandages," Soraya told me.

"How did the scar look?" She shook her head as to say it was pretty bad. So the scar must be fucked up. But it didn't matter. I didn't care that he had a scar. I was happy that he was alive and with us.

"You have to call your job," I reminded Soraya.

"I'm going to call and use a personal day," she replied. "I'm calling in a few."

M.J. fell asleep again at that point.

"I have to call my job again and speak to my supervisor," I told her. "I spoke to Dr. Patel again and he told me that M.J. should be alright. He sounded real confident when he said it too."

She offered me some of her Doritos but the pack of pretzels I ate satisfied me. I didn't really have an appetite anyway. M.J. was asleep so we went outside the hospital to make our phone calls. We both had our cell phones and made our calls to family and friends. I called Chuck to find out the latest information.

"What's up?" I asked. "I need you to pick me and Soraya up."

"When?"

"In about a half an hour," I responded.

"Alright."

"Anything new?"

"Not yet. But don't worry. We're gonna get that motherfucka Drugs."

"No question," I replied. "We'll be right by the Emergency entrance when you come get us."

"Alright, I'll be there in a half," Chuck replied.

"Later on then." Soraya was still on her phone so I returned some other calls. After about 15 or 20 minutes, she finished all of her calls.

"Chuck is going to pick us up in a few," I told her.

"No," she responded. "I'm going to wait here for your mother. She said she's going to be here in about an hour or so. Then I'll take a cab home to shower and change."

"But we're getting a ride. Why do you want to wait and then take a cab home later?"

"Because if M.J. wakes up, I want someone to always be there and it should be a family member. I'm going upstairs now," she said seeming real tense.

Chuck pulled up in front of us right then and turned down the music in his car. He came out of his car and gave me a pound.

"How are you doing?" he asked Soraya while giving her a hug and kiss on her cheek.

"I'm alright," she responded coldly.

"How's M.J.?"

"He's stable right now. You know, we just have to pray for him. I'm going back upstairs now. Are you coming to see him now?"

"No, not right now," Chuck responded.

"I'll come see him later on. What times are visiting hours?"

"I'm not sure what time it starts but it ends at 8 o'clock," she replied. "I think the hours are 2 to 8 or 3 to 8. Something like that."

"Is my Pops going to watch Brian?" I asked Soraya.

"Yeah." I gave her a hug and kiss and whispered in her ear, "Call me if anything happens or if you need anything."

"I will," she said. "What time are you coming back?"

"I don't know," I replied.

"I'm going to shower and then I have some shit to do."

"What shit?"

"Some shit," I told her in a tone that made her know not to push the issue.

"Alright," she said. "Do what you gotta do." She knew more or less what I was talking about.

"Love you," I said to her.

"Love you." As she walked back into the hospital, Chuck and I got into his car and drove off.

I had the mad screw face as I sat quietly looking out the window. I looked at people going about their business. I wondered what kind of problems they were going through or had in their lives. As we drove through the neighborhood streets, I looked in peoples' faces and tried to see if there were indications of the problems or adversities that they were dealing with in their lives. I felt that if anyone looked in my face, directly in my eyes, they would see all that I was feeling. All my pain, desperation and anger would be plainly seen. I would be unable to hide it. That's why I wondered if anyone was going through the same trials that I was facing, or was it that they were just able to mask it better. Maybe they've dealt with adversity more than I.

I had a lot of uncertainties. One thing that I was certain of was that there was going to be retribution for what happened. I could not wait. Chuck, sensing how I was feeling, didn't try to talk to me. I didn't want to talk. We pulled up in front of our building where a bunch of the fellas and other people from the neighborhood were gathered. All eyes seemed to target me as Chucks' car came to a stop. I knew I wouldn't get in my house anytime soon as everyone would want to wish me and my family well; ask how we were doing, and ask what we planned to do about it. All that was well and good but at that time I didn't want to deal with it.

"Oh shit," I said in part frustration and fatigue. "I don't want to deal with this shit."

"I'll take care of it," Chuck responded. As I walked towards the building, all I heard was people calling my name from different directions. A lot of people were talking to me at the same time. They were giving me pounds and hugs.

"Sorry to hear about M.J."

"How are you doing?" The comments flew at me from the crowd of mostly well-wishers. Of course there were people there who were just nosy. Don't get me wrong; I did appreciate the concern and kind words. But please, I needed to shower, shit and shave. I needed to get some sleep. I answered some of the questions as quickly as I could, because the questions were coming rapid fire one by one. I looked at Chuck like, "I thought you said you would take care of this shit?"

"Yo," Chuck said to me, loud enough for the crowd to hear. "You have to get some rest before you go back to the hospital."

"You're right. I'm going upstairs now, thanks."

"I'll see ya'll later," I told the people in the crowd before we walked into the building.

"Wait here a minute," I told Chuck as I walked into my moms' house. "I gotta make sure my mom is dressed."

He waited for me in the hallway.

"Mom, you dressed?" I yelled.

"Daddy!" Brian screamed excitedly.

"What's up baby boy?" I asked as he ran into my arms for a hug. "Nothing. How's M.J.?" My mother walked out from the back and she was dressed.

"Chuck's outside," I told her.

"Tell him to come inside," she responded. I opened the door and told Chuck to come inside.

"How's M.J., Daddy?" Brian asked with more urgency.

"He's OK," I told him. "He asked for you. He wanted to know where you were." I knew telling Brian that would make him feel good.

"When can I see him?" He asked with a smile.

"I have to find out from Mommy." I said.

"Call her now," he demanded.

"I'll call her a little later, alright?"

Chuck and my mother were talking to each other while Brian tried to persuade me to find out when he could see M.J.

"Where's Dad?" I asked my mother.

"He went to the store. I'm waiting for him to come back so I can go to the hospital. He's going to watch Brian unless you're going to take him with you now."

I shook my head no. Then she said, "Go and get my keys from off of my dresser please."

As I walked to the back followed by Brian, who still wanted me to call Soraya, something struck me as strange. My mother didn't bring anything up about M.J. or ask how I was doing. I just figured it was because of everything that happened and she wanted to get to the hospital to see M.J. for herself.

I brought her the keys and said to Chuck, "I'm leaving." He got up, said bye to my mother and walked towards the door with me.

"Brian," I said. "I'm leaving now but I'm going to call Mommy later and I'll let you know when you can see M.J."

"Can I go with you?" Brian asked me.

"Not now. I have some things to do but I'll come back for you later on."

"Aw man," he said. "I want to go."

"Not now Brian. I have some important things to take care of."

"More important than me?" he asked. I kneeled down, looked him straight in his eyes.and said. "There is nothing in this world more important than you or M.J. or anyone else in this family. Ya'll are the most important people in my life, understand? But right now, I have to take care of some other things. If I could take you with me I would. But you can't come with me right now. I'll come for you later, OK?"

"OK," he said.

"Alright Mom, I'll see you later at the hospital." She nodded but I could tell that she was preoccupied.

"I want to go with you Daddy!" That's all I heard being yelled as I walked out the door. "I want to go with you Daddy!!"

On the elevator I said to Chuck, "Do me a favor and find something out. I'm going to get some sleep but call me if something comes up. I don't care what it is, call me and wake me up."

"I got you," he said as I got off on my floor. All that I kept thinking and all that consumed me was revenge. It was about to be on.

Chapter 8

The phone rang and startled me out of a restful sleep. I jumped up out of bed and opened the curtains to bring the afternoon sun into the darkened room. That way I could see who was calling by checking the Caller ID box next to my phone. It was Roberto's cell phone number.

"Roberto, What's up?" I asked with fatigue in my voice.

"Sorry to wake you up," Roberto responded. "Chuck told me to call you, no matter what, if we found something out. And we did."

"What happened?" I asked anxiously.

"This motherfucka Drugs is at the basketball courts right now."

"These courts or Woodson courts?"

"Woodson," he replied. "Chuck drove by there and saw Tyrell. Tyrell told him that Drugs was on the courts. Chuck told Tyrell to stay there and make sure to let him know if Drugs left. I was right outside when Chuck pulled up in front and told me to call you and let you know. Chuck talked to the crew and told them what was up and that we were going over there now. He went to his house to get the burner. He told me to call you to come outside so we could go over there. So let's go."

"How long ago did all of this happen?" I asked.

"Just now."

"No, what I'm asking is how long ago did Tyrell see Drugs in the park?"

"Well, Chuck pulled up in front of the building about 10 minutes ago and he went to his house about 5 minutes ago."

"Alright, I'm coming down now."

"Later then," he said. I hung up and quickly threw on some sweatpants and a black t-shirt and ran out the door. I walked out the building and my boys were out there waiting for me. Just a few hours earlier, the crowd of people outside my building were wishing my family and I well. Now the crowd out there was ready to cause damage.

There had been an underlying tension between people from Crown Heights Plaza and Woodson Projects for a long time. It's said that the beef started many years earlier at a basketball tournament game in Woodson. I heard that the teams from both Woodson and the Plaza were in the championship game. There was a lot of rough play. Each team was accusing each other of dirty play. There were a lot of questionable calls by the refs. Tensions were high all throughout the game and the score was close till the end.

There was this guy from the Plaza called Boogie, because he had mad handle with the basketball. With under a minute left in the game, Boogie crossed over someone from Woodson and went up for a lay-up and supposedly caught an elbow. He went down hard to the ground but no foul was called. Woodson won the game by two points. There was some pushing and shoving between the players on the court right after the game ended. That sparked fights between people from the Plaza and Woodson on the bleachers and outside of the courts. Eventually there was a shootout right across the street from the park. This all happened right after the game. A teenaged girl from Woodson got shot in her leg from that initial shootout.

Ever since that night, the beef's been on. Dudes from Woodson would come around here and get shot at, stabbed or jumped. If dudes from the Plaza went to Woodson it would be the same shit happening over there. That's why the tournaments were shut down after that game. The Plaza security was around when all this shit was happening but there were only a few of them patrolling the entire Plaza. Quite honestly they were shook themselves. They'd call the N.Y.P.D quickly before they would try and stop some shit that was going down. It was so bad that dudes from the Plaza and Woodson, who went to the same local high school, would have fights in and around the school. There would be crews, 20 people deep each, fighting each other.

It was crazy back then. I had plenty of fights throughout my high school years representing the Plaza. Shit had calmed down and gotten safer around here because of more Plaza security being hired. There was also more of a presence by the N.Y.P.D. The people in the neighborhood complained, had community meetings and spoke with congressmen and community leaders. Slowly but surely the neighborhood got safer to the point it was before the recent rash of violence. Even though dudes from the Plaza and Woodson go to each other's neighborhood now without the beef from the past, an uneasy truce remained. The underlying tension never went away.

Chuck and Roberto were already in front of the building with the rest of the fellas. Chuck looked at me and asked, "You ready?"

"Hell yeah, let's go," I responded. I hadn't had those feelings of excitement and trepidation in a long time, but it felt different. As all fifteen of us packed into three cars, I realized that the fury built up in me was boiled to the point that it clouded my judgment. It was a rage, as I'd never felt before. There were times that I knew what I wanted to do to Drugs was not in anyone's best interest. but my craving for revenge dominated my thoughts, feelings and better judgment.

In Chuck's car, it was Chuck, Roberto, Mark, Jay and I.

"I haven't seen Lou or heard about anyone seeing him since yesterday," Roberto said.

"Where's the burner?" I asked.

"Under your seat," Chuck said as he pointed to the passenger side seat. I reached under the seat and pulled out the 9 millimeter.

"Yo, I got mine too Malik," Mark said to me referring to his gun. I just looked at him and nodded my head. We were a block away from the basketball courts at Woodson as we parked the cars. I put the gun in my waistband and we all marched towards the courts. As we got close enough to the courts, I could see about twenty people on it. Drugs was sitting on the bleachers talking on his cell phone. There were six people sitting around him and some of his workers were running a half court game.

Tyrell gave me a pound and said, "He's been here for awhile but Trip hasn't." Drugs was sitting there chillin', while my son was laid up in the hospital. That motherfucka was going to get fucked up.

As we invaded the court, the basketball game stopped and Drugs and his people stood up. I was so determined on what I was going to do that I didn't pay attention to anyone else there but Drugs.

"What's up motherfucka?" Drugs asked me in a hostile tone as he came off the bleachers. As I got closer to him, his people stood in front of me to keep me at a distance.

"What the fuck you mean?" I yelled. "You shot my son motherfucka, that's what's up."

"I didn't shoot nobody motherfucka?" he yelled back. When he said that shit to me, I moved towards Drugs and one of his boys put his hands on me and gave me a little push.

"Get the fuck off of him!" Chuck said angrily as he mushed that guy in his face. A stocky Puerto Rican kid, who was to my right, threw a punch that caught me above my eye. That punch dazed me for a few seconds. Everyone was fighting at that point. It was a fuckin' free for all. There were punches being thrown everywhere. The dude that hit me was saying something to me but I didn't hear what. I knew he was talking shit though. My senses came back quickly and it wasn't a moment too soon because he threw another punch. I was ready for that punch and I moved out of the way. I countered with a right cross of my own followed by a left hook that put him on his ass. He had a surprised look on his face like 'Oh shit!'

Then someone put me in a chokehold from behind. I grabbed and pulled on the person's right arm. I was trying to relieve the pressure he was putting on my throat. Then one of my people punched the dude that was choking me because he let go of me and went down. He was out cold. I looked at him for a couple of seconds and then looked at who punched him. It was Tyrell. I then turned my attention back to finding Drugs. At that very moment the sounds of police sirens coming closer filled the air. Everyone on the court scattered in different directions.

Everything happened so quickly. Someone who lives in one of the apartments overlooking the basketball courts must've seen a large group of men congregating and decided trouble was about to jump off. In this case, they were correct. They must've called the police. That could've been the only way that the cops were on the way so quickly. I looked to find Drugs again in between all the people running, but I didn't see him.

Roberto grabbed my arm and said, "We have to go." The urgency in his voice was apparent.

"Let's go, Po-Po is coming." We ran to the cars as the sirens came even closer. At Chuck's car, I put the burner back under the passenger seat.

"I'm walking back to the block."

"Alright," he said. He knew exactly why. If the cops saw a carload of guys leaving the scene of a disturbance, that car was getting stopped, because of the recent violence, a lot of cops would be there shortly. It was only Chuck, Jay and I in the car. Mark and Roberto must've jetted off. The rest of the crew's cars were already gone.

"Jay, let's go," I said. Jay got out of the car and I told him and Chuck to meet me at my house in an hour. Chuck pulled off and Jay and I walked in separate directions back to the block.

Chapter 9

"This shit ain't over," I said angrily, an hour after the incident on the basketball court. Chuck, Roberto and I were at my house. Jay hadn't shown up so we didn't know what happened to him at that point. Mark went to his house.

"You saw how that motherfucka didn't even care that he shot M.J.?" I said. "I'm gonna get him."

It didn't matter to me that I got punched or that I almost got choked out. It only mattered that I wanted to fuck Drugs up and I was real close but my opportunity was wasted.

He was probably going to have more of his crew around him and this time they were going to be squeezing off shots. I had to watch out for those punks. I wasn't trying to end up like Mack and Rick. I definitely couldn't have them doing something to my family. The incident at the courts made me realize that I couldn't go about it the same way. I had to be smarter, and I had an idea of how I wanted to do it. I started telling Chuck and them what the plan was but at that moment Soraya walked in the house.

"What's up baby?" I asked. "Are you alright? How's M.J.?"

"I'm fine," she replied sounding exhausted. "M.J. is the same. He's still stable. He was awake for a while longer today. Your mom and I talked to him. He asked for you of course. That's it. I'm going to go back later on after I get some sleep." Chuck and Roberto got the hint.

"Alright, we're out," said Chuck taking the hint. "Call me when ya'll are ready to go back to the hospital." Soraya and I said, "Later" to them and they bounced.

"You hungry?" I asked her. "I'm going to order something."

"What are you ordering?"

"What do you want?" I asked.

"Chinese. Let me get General Tso's chicken," she responded. "I spoke to Carla a little while ago and she told me about the argument she had on the phone with Rodney today."

"What about now?" I asked.

"She told him that she might be spending the night here so she could visit M.J. and go to work from here."

"Why is she even explaining herself to him if she said that they wasn't together anymore?" I asked.

"That's what I asked her. She said she just wanted him to know. I told her that was a dumb ass reason." I agreed. "She said again that it was over with Rodney and she wasn't going to get back with him," Soraya continued.

"But anyway, she told him that she was spending the night here and he started beefin'.

He started accusing her of fucking someone around here. He called her a whore and said if he finds out who she's fuckin' he's going to kill him and her. Since she was at work she couldn't really argue back like she would have if she were at home. But she said she told him to get all his shit and leave. By the weekend she's going to change the locks on the front door."

I looked at Soraya, took in everything she told me and said, "I'll call Rodney and talk to him." Soraya looked surprised that I offered to do that.

"What are you going to say to him?"

"Don't worry, I'll take care of it," I replied.

"Just get his cell number from Carla and I'll call tonight because he's buggin' out. I'll talk to him."

"Alright, I'll get the number," Soraya said. Then I told her about the incident at the basketball courts and her reaction was, "You should have killed him." I didn't expect that from her. But her reaction just let me know that she was down for whatever I decided to do. She got on the phone and got Rodney's phone number from Carla.

"Here it is," she said.

"Let me know what happens so I can tell Carla."

"Alright."

"I'm going to take a shower now," she told me. As Soraya took a shower, I called Chuck.

"Yo, I was just going to call you," Chuck told me. "I just spoke to Eric and he told me some shit."

"What?" I asked. "He said that Trip is fuckin' Yvette."

"Yvette who? Drugs girl Yvette?" I asked surprised by the revelation. "Get the fuck outta here."

"That shit is real," Chuck replied. "He said that they've been fuckin' for a while but it's been on the low. Eric didn't even find out about it until yesterday. You know that snitch would've told the whole neighborhood if he knew. So when Mack and Lou was talking that shit to Yvette, she went to tell Trip what happened first before she told Drugs. So Trip went with his people and handled Mack and Rick. But Drugs didn't know anything about it until after Mack was shot. Eric said Drugs was pissed that Trip did that without his OK and letting him know the whole situation first. So they were arguing and Drugs wanted to know why Trip did it. Trip told him some bullshit. But after Mack got shot, Drugs had to go after Rick and Lou because he knew that they would come after him. That's why he had some of his workers driving his car around. It was a decoy. He wanted people to think it was him driving around. You know that no one can see inside his truck because of the dark tints. So he wanted to see if the cops would stop the car or if motherfuckas were going to try some shit. It's lucky he did because Lou would have shot him if he were driving around himself. So initially Drugs had nothing to do with it. But he knew what was going to happen to Rick and Lou before it happened."

"It doesn't matter how much he knew or didn't know. I'm getting all those motherfuckas," I told Chuck. "I'm glad you told me that. It's good to know. We're going to use that information to our advantage. I need you to find out where Trip is going to be tonight and tomorrow. It's important Chuck. If you need to have someone follow him, then do it."

"Done," he responded. "What's the plan?"

I told him my plan and he said, "It may work, it all depends..." Before he could finish his sentence, Soraya called me.

"Malik, is the food here yet?"

"No, not yet," I replied. "Chuck, don't forget. I'm going to call you back. Later." We hung up. I called the Chinese restaurant again to find out what was taking them so long. Then I made another phone call. After that call I felt kind of relieved. Soraya walked out of the bathroom wearing just a towel. As she was putting her panties on, I told her that the deliveryman was on his way. I also told her about the conversation I just had and how relieved I was. I told her what my plan was and she said, "Be careful. Whatever you do just be careful."

"I will," I responded. The doorbell rang. The Chinese food finally arrived. As I put the food on the table, I said, "I'm going to call Carla now. I have to speak to her about tonight." She nodded her head as she sat down to eat.

"Carla, what's up?" I asked. "Are you coming to visit M.J. today?"

"No," she replied. "I'm more than likely going there tomorrow. Why?"

"Are you going to spend the night?" I asked.

"Yes," she replied.

"Good. I need a favor from you." I broke everything down and she said, "Alright, but don't let anything come back to me."

"It won't," I assured her. "Trust me. Just make sure that you spend a few days here."

"Alright," she said again. "I'm going to call Rodney now," I continued.

"You remember what to say to him right?"

"Yes."

"Good," I said. "You want to speak to Soraya?"

Soraya was all in her food and with a mouth full of food said, "Tell her I'll call her back."

"Did you hear that?" I asked Carla. "She's eating and said she'll call you back." I told Carla that I would see her tomorrow and proceeded to kill my chicken and broccoli. But I only ate about half my plate before my stomach was full.

Soraya went to take a nap and I dialed Rodney's cell phone number.

"Rodney, it's Malik," I announced as he picked up the phone. He stayed quiet for a few seconds. "What's up?" He said in a way that implied that he didn't know why the fuck I was calling him. I had a serious tone in my voice that made him know this wasn't a social call. "I'm calling to let you know about this dude from around here that's been trying to kick it to Carla."

"What?" He asked with anger in his voice.

"There's this drug dealer named Trip that's been kickin' it hard to Carla," I told him. "Before you get pissed, she didn't want him talking to her. She told him she had a man and wasn't interested but he kept talking to her anyway. So I stepped to him and told him that she already had a man."

"So you saw him trying to talk to her all that time and didn't say anything right away?" he asked me.

"I wasn't there for the whole conversation. I had just come around the way. I saw him talking to her and she looked uncomfortable. She was trying to ignore him but he was in her face. When I saw that, I stepped to him."

"Why was she just standing there letting that motherfucka talk to her?" he asked.

"It wasn't like that. Carla was outside the building with M.J. and Brian. She was sitting, by herself, watching the kids play when that motherfucka started kickin' it to her. When I stepped to him, that motherfucka started beefin'. He was getting loud and running his mouth so we were going to fight. My people broke it up though. But he was still talking a lot of shit. He said he was going to talk to Carla whenever he saw her and anyone that didn't like it would get blasted. So he was basically disrespecting Carla, you and me. He said he was going to make Carla his girl. He pulled out a wad of money and said he would take care of her and she wouldn't have to worry about anything. He said that if she had any kids, he would take care of them like they were his own. But like I said, I wasn't there for the whole conversation. Carla told me the rest of what he said to her."

"So she could've been talking to him and she played it off when you came around," Rodney stated.

"No," I told him. "When I first saw him talking to her, she didn't see me. She was trying to ignore him and was kind of waving him off but he wasn't trying to hear that. I finally just brought Carla and the kids upstairs. I don't know if she told you all of this or not. She said you would flip or do something crazy. But if you did decide to do something, I wouldn't blame you. He was real disrespectful. Carla didn't do anything wrong and I make sure that guys don't talk to her or bother her when she's around here. She doesn't talk to anyone. She keeps to herself. The only people she talks to around here are me and Soraya. I don't like that motherfucka anyway from before that shit with Carla. Me and him had words before."

"What's his name again?" He asked in a serious and angry tone.

"Trip," I told him.

Rodney was quiet most of the time while I told him all that shit. I could tell he was pissed from his heavy breathing and the way he asked the few questions that he did.

"Whatever you want to do to this motherfucka, I'm with you. I got your back. I got my people watching him right now. They're just waiting on my word because I told them I was going to speak to you and you'd probably want to do that motherfucka."

By telling Rodney that, I knew his temper would get the better of him. "Yeah fuck that," he exclaimed. "Let's do that motherfucka. I don't give a fuck who he is, I'm gonna do that motherfucka." I knew that by telling him I had my people watching Trip, it would make it seem easier for him. Basically, Rodney is a lazy dude. I made everything easy for him. I dropped it in his lap. Attacking certain people's ego or pride can be just as effective as punching them in their damn face.

"Shit is hot around here because there's been a few shootings around here recently." I explained to Rodney. "So if you really want to do something to that motherfucka, you should do it today or tomorrow. Trip is involved in some of the shootings around here and he's probably going on the run. So if you really want to do this, tell me now. If you don't, I'm going to tell my people to stop watching him. But personally, if some dude tried that shit with Soraya, I would shoot him. That's me though."

"That's my word," he said, "I'm gonna do that motherfucka."

"You got a burner?" I asked him.

"No doubt."

"You driving your car when you come out here?"

"Yeah."

"I'm going to call my people now and find out what the deal is," I told him. "Almost every Tuesday night he goes to Club Cocoa's. That's a strip club around here. More than likely you can catch him there."

"Alright, call me and let me know," Rodney said sounding real hyped. I hung up from Rodney and sat on my couch thinking about everything. Needless to say, everything I told Rodney, about Trip trying to talk to Carla, never happened. I made all that shit up as part of the plan that was in motion. I had so much more shit to do but I wasn't going to stop. After a short nap, Soraya and I got ready to see M.J. Phase two of my plan was about to begin.

Chapter 10

"It's good to see you M.J." I told him as I gave him a hug and kiss on his forehead. "Are you feeling better?"

He nodded his head. I could tell that he was still in a lot of pain. He was also probably scared and confused, as were Soraya and I. That's so much for a 5 year old to deal with. He was still on medication for the pain and it made him sluggish. I hated seeing him like that.

"Ma," I said to my mother, "Chuck is going to take you home when you're ready. He's downstairs waiting."

"Why didn't he come see M.J.?" she asked me. "He was going to but he said he didn't want to see M.J. like that."

"That's ridiculous," she replied unconvinced by my explanation. "I'm leaving in a little while."

"I'm going to be leaving with you," I replied.

"Already?"

"Yeah, I have some things to do."

"What things are you into?" She asked. "What are you doing?" She was clearly agitated.

"I have some things I have to take care of," I replied with slight attitude of my own. She gave me a dirty look but left it alone. I understood why she was upset. She felt that I should've stayed with my son but I had to make shit right.

As she turned her attention back to M.J., I said to Soraya, "I forgot to tell you that Carla's not coming to see M.J. today. She'll see him tomorrow."

After another 20 minutes or so, I looked at my watch and said, "It's time to go." Soraya was staying with M.J. so I was basically talking to my moms. We exchanged our last hugs and kisses with M.J. and Soraya and we made our way out.

Outside the hospital Chuck sat in his car with the seat leaned back.

We walked to the car and Chuck said, "Hey Ms. Ford."

"Hello Chuck," my mother answered coldly. "You should have come up to see M.J."

"Ms. Ford," he said. "I can't see him like that. I don't like seeing kids hurt."

"Uh Huh," my mom said. She stayed quiet for the rest of the trip back home. After we dropped her off, Chuck asked, "Why didn't Soraya come with you?" He waited all that time before he asked because he was probably conscious of my mother being upset with him.

"She's going to take a cab back," I responded.

"Are you sure?" he asked. "I'll go pick her up if you want."

"Nah, she'll be cool. She has her razor and cell phone. She'll be alright." As I began to listen to my voicemail on my cell, Chuck said, "I spoke to Jay."

I put my index finger up indicating for him to hold on a minute. I opened up the glove compartment and took out a pen and wrote down a phone number. I hung up and said to Chuck, "I got the phone number."

"Good," he responded. "Like I said, I spoke to Jay."

"Yeah? What's he saying?"

"Nothing, he's chillin'. He made it home and he's alright. He wants to know what's next."

"We'll let him know," I told him as I dialed Carla's number. "Carla, what's up?" I asked.

"I'm OK," she replied.

"Did you speak to Rodney?"

"No."

"Remember what I told you to say to him if you do speak to him."

"Yeah, I know what to say," was her response.

I told Carla about the conversation I had earlier with Rodney. She wasn't surprised by his reaction.

"I told you he would react like that."

"I know," I responded.

"You coming out here tomorrow right?"

"Yeah."

"Get a pen," I told her. "I have the phone number for you to call." After a brief moment, she came back to the phone and said, "Alright, give me the number." I gave her the number and asked her to make the call right then.

"OK," she said. "Tell me again what you want me to say."

"Tell Drugs that you're calling to let him know that Trip is fuckin' Yvette. Tell him that's the reason that Trip shot Mack in the first place. Yvette told Trip about what happened with Mack first and he got pissed. Then tell him that Trip and Yvette been fuckin' for a while and they've been playing him. Let him know that you didn't feel that it was right especially since it brought about so much trouble in the neighborhood. If he asks who you are and how you got his cell number, tell him that you're a friend of Yvette's and you remembered the number from the times that she's called him in front of you. Of course don't tell him your name. If it works correctly, Drugs will be upset with Trip and Yvette and check your story to see if it's true. The thing is, I need for you to call him now."

"Alright," she said.

"How's your daughter?" I asked. "Is she still staying with your mom?"

"Yes. I didn't want her around while Rodney and I have been arguing."

"I hear that," I said. "That's good though. She doesn't need to be around that bullshit with Rodney."

"Yeah, I know." She said and then asked, "How's Soraya?"

"She's the same."

"Is she there?"

"No. She's at the hospital with M.J. I just came from there. I'm here with Chuck."

"Tell her I said hello," Chuck said to me.

"Chuck said to tell you hello," I relayed to Carla.

"Tell him I said. 'What's the deal?'" Carla replied. I gave Chuck the message and then Carla asked me, "How's M.J.?"

"He's a little better." I didn't want to talk about that so I changed the subject. "I'm going to call you back in an hour to find out how it went."

"Alright," she replied.

As soon as we hung up, Chuck said, "Drugs is going to be pissed when Carla tells him about Yvette."

"I know," I responded with a slight smirk. I then dialed Rodney's phone number and got right to the point.

"Rodney, I just want to say right off that I'm with you tomorrow for getting Trip. But if you're going to shoot him, that's on you. I'm not shooting anyone. I have my family living here and after shit goes down, I'll still be here. I'm not trying to jeopardize my family's safety.

I have a plan for you and your people to get him but I can't be involved like that. I ain't shooting anyone so let's get that straight. I can't control what you do and you're going to do what you're going to do. That's on you."

"I hear what you're saying, Malik," Rodney said. I interrupted him and continued with what I was saying.

"I don't blame you for being mad though. That motherfucka Trip was mad disrespectful. He said no one was gonna stop him from talking to Carla. He said if you or anyone stepped to him, he would blast em. And he definitely would shoot you. He's sick in the head like that. If you stepped to him, he wouldn't try and beat your ass, he'd shoot you. So I don't blame you for whatever you want to do. You know what I'm saying?"

"I hear you," Rodney replied.

"I understand what you're saying about you living there and not wanting shit coming back to you and your family. But like you said, I'm gonna do what I gotta do. I ain't letting no one play me. I don't give a fuck if he's the biggest hustler on your block or the biggest hustler in Brooklyn. That motherfucka is getting fucked up. This shit ain't a game."

"So do you want me to set shit up for you or not?" I asked.

"Yeah, no question. Do you still have your people watching him?"

"Yeah. It's on you now."

"Let's do it then," he said. I told Rodney how everything was going down the next night then we got off the phone. We had been sitting in Chuck's car for a while making phone calls and I was tired. The next day was going to be another long one. I had to get sleep to be mentally and physically prepared. I had to call Carla back.

"I'm tired as fuck," I told Chuck.

"So go get some sleep," he replied.

"I have to call Carla back," I said.

"I'll call her back," he offered.

"Alright cool. Let me know what she said." Before he could respond, my phone rang.

"Speak of the devil," I said to Chuck as I showed him the number on my cell phone. "What's up, Carla?" I asked as I answered the phone. "Did you speak to him?"

"Yeah," she replied. "I just got off the phone with him. When he answered his phone, I said I was a friend of Yvette and I was calling to let him know that Yvette and Trip were fucking. He asked who was I because he said he knows all of Yvette's friends. I said I didn't want to say who I was. I could tell he was trying to recognize my voice."

"Do you think he did?" I asked.

"I doubt it," she replied. "Anyway, he asked how I got his number and I told him that Yvette has called him in front of me before, and I remembered the number. Then he asked again who I was and I told him again I was a friend of Yvette and I wasn't going to tell him my name. I could tell by his voice that he didn't believe me at first. But when I gave more specific details he started believing more. I told him everything that I was supposed to."

"And what else was he saying?" I asked.

"He didn't say too much, except for what I already told you he said. He was just listening for the most part. Then he said he would look into it. Then we hung up. We weren't on the phone that long. Even though he sounded like he believed me somewhat, I could also tell that he was skeptical. Here I am, some stranger calling him on his cell telling him his girl is fuckin' his right hand man. For all he knows, I'm just some hater trying to fuck his thing up."

"But you know what?" I asked, "The purpose of telling him all that is to occupy his mind so he has one more thing to think about and contend with. Also I want to cause dissension between Drugs and Trip. That's the bottom line. Regardless of how he may have sounded, he's going to confront them about it. There's no question about that. There's no question he's going to look into it. That's what I want. Along with all the other shit he's dealing with now, I want him to deal with it even more.

You know what I'm sayin'? Fuck him. Anyway, good lookin' out Carla."

"No problem," she said. "I hope everything works out."

"Yeah, me too," I said. "Did you hear from Rodney?"

"He called and left me a message saying he had to talk to me and to call him back." She responded. "I ain't calling him back though."

"Good," I said. "What time are you coming around tomorrow?"

"After work," she told me.

"Good, I'll speak to you then. Later."

"Bye."

"Chuck," I said, "These past few days, I've spent a lot of time on my cell phone. I know I've gone over my monthly minutes."

"I hear you," Chuck said. "What happened with Carla and Drugs?" I told Chuck what happened and he said, "Everything looks like it's working so far."

"So far," I said, stepping out of the car to stretch my legs. "I'm about to go upstairs," I continued. "Are you ready for tomorrow?"

"No question. It's gonna go down."

"Get the fellas and everything ready," I told him. I gave Chuck a pound and with fatigue kicking my ass, I went to my house filled with anticipation for the next day's events.

Chapter 11

As I went into my apartment, I went straight for the answering machine. Soraya left me a message a couple of hours earlier. She said that M.J. seemed like he was getting better. I hoped it wasn't just wishful thinking on her part but that he was actually getting better. She also said that M.J. asked for me. That motivated me more for going through with the plan. I needed everything to work. I went through the rest of the messages, took my shower and fell out.

I woke up at a little after 8:00 am. I was still tired but I was anxious to get the day going. I hurriedly washed up, dressed and ate cereal before going outside. Roberto and Eric were talking outside of the building. I walked towards them and gave them pounds.

"What's up?" I asked.

"Chillin'," they replied.

"Guess what Eric was just telling me?" Roberto asked me.

"What?" I asked.

"He saw Bam driving around with Drugs."

"Get the fuck outta here," I said with disbelief in my voice.

"Yeah, it's true," Eric said. "Last night, I saw Bam in the passenger seat of Drugs Benz. They drove right by me on Prospect Street. The windows were open so I saw him clearly."

"Did they see you?" I asked.

"Nah, I doubt it," he replied.

"I walked out the Chinese restaurant as they drove by. Trust me, it was Bam. I looked right at him and I was buggin' that he would be with Drugs. I didn't think they were cool like that."

I looked at Roberto and said angrily, "You see what I mean about that bitch-ass Bam? That's why I don't like that motherfucka. My son is laid up in the fuckin' hospital right now and this motherfucka is driving around with the dude who's responsible. Fuck Bam. Fuck that punk ass motherfucka."

"Relax," Roberto said to me. "Don't even stress it."

"I'm not stressing shit," I said. "But don't ever ask me why I don't squash our beef. I'm not squashing a motherfuckin' thing. Now you know why I hate that motherfucka."

Eric changed the subject by saying, "I heard about that beef you had with Drugs at the courts at Woodson."

"Yeah," I replied. "I was going to beat his ass but he had all his boys in between us."

"You ain't afraid he's gonna do something to you because of that incident?" Eric asked.

"No," I said defiantly, "I'm not. If he tries some shit, he'd better kill me. If he does, he knows my people from the Plaza will get him. It'll be a war out here. He knows that. My people will have Woodson Projects hotter than it is now and he doesn't want that. That's bad for his business. When I do see Drugs again, I'm going to beat his ass. You can tell him that. My son is up in the hospital right now, fighting for his life with a big ass scar in his stomach because of him."

"I hear you," Eric said. Eric is a little snitch. I wanted him to tell Drugs what I had said. "We have to go," I said to Roberto.

"Where ya'll headed?" Eric asked.

"We're going to Jersey," Roberto answered.

"What ya'll gonna do out there?" Eric asked. "I'm gonna pick my aunt up and take her to the hospital to see my son. Then I have to drive her back afterwards," I told him.

"So we're going to be gone for a minute."

"How is your son?" Eric asked.

I looked at him for a few seconds and with a hint of attitude I said, "He's OK." I didn't feel like answering that question at that time. And I especially didn't want to answer Eric.

"Yo, we're out." Roberto said. He saw that I didn't want to talk to Eric anymore. I looked Eric directly in his eyes and gave him a pound. I didn't know if he could tell or not but I didn't like him. I never really did. I didn't like that he always talked about people's business. He didn't really care how M.J. was. He just asked to be asking. He didn't care what my answer was. I don't like people who show fake concern. I'd rather they not say anything. The look I gave him at that time reflected my dislike and disgust for him. As Roberto and I walked away, he asked me, "What happened?"

"When he brought up M.J., it pissed me off. That motherfucka don't care about M.J.,

He's just nosy. I didn't want him bringing M.J. up."

"You were pissed," Roberto said half laughing.

"You damn right," I told him. "You think he could tell?"

"I don't know," he replied. "But fuck it."

"By telling Eric that we were going to Jersey, no one's going to expect to see us around."

"Yeah, that shit is slick," Roberto said.

"Yeah. But we gotta keep it moving. We gotta find out what Trip and them are up to and whether he's going to Cocoa's tonight. I want to call Rodney and let him know what time to come out here. When we get to Cal's house, I'm going to call Chuck to see what's up." Cal is one of our people that live in the Plaza. We were out of Eric's sight as we cut to Cal's building. We rang his doorbell.

"Who is it?" Cal yelled through the door.

"It's Malik and Roberto," I replied. I heard the sound of the peephole being opened and then closed. Let me explain what kind of person Cal is. Cal is a paranoid motherfucka who doesn't really trust people. He's always fighting and has a lot of beef with people. It took years for us to be cool and have the level of trust that we had. He always told us that him not growing up with his father made him the person that he was, referring to the trouble he always seemed to be in.

That being said, it wasn't hard understanding Cal's philosophy on answering his door. If someone rings his doorbell, he'll yell for whoever it is to identify themselves while he's away from the door. That way if someone decided to shoot through the door, he wouldn't get hit. Then he'd look through the peephole. We know people who've been shot through their doors so it wasn't like it was something new. He was at the basketball courts with us the day earlier when we confronted Drugs. After he looked at us through the peephole, he unlocked the many locks on his door. He cracked open the door and peeked his head out. Then he opened the door wider to let us in.

"What's up?" I asked Cal. His response was a nod of his in acknowledgment. As we walked in, we noticed he had his 9-millimeter to his side. He locked the door back up and I asked him if I could make some phone calls.

"Go ahead," he replied. "What's good?" Cal asked us.

"I can't call it," Roberto replied. I dialed Chuck's number as Roberto and Cal started talking shit to each other about which team was better in Madden Football.

"Chuck," I said as he answered his phone, "Where are you?"

"I'm with a couple of the fellas," Chuck replied. "Taking care of this business and getting shit ready."

"I saw Eric today," I said. "What's he saying?" Asked Chuck.

"You know how he is. Motherfucka got on my nerves."

"What happened?"

"He asked me about M.J. and that pissed me off. You know he don't give a fuck about M.J."

"Yeah, I know" Chuck agreed. "He also told me that he saw Bam driving around with Drugs."

"Oh yeah?" he asked. "Where did he see them?"

"He said he saw them in front of the Chinese restaurant on Prospect Street. He said he was positive that it was Bam."

"And what did you say?" Chuck asked.

"I broke," I replied. "I told him that's why I didn't like Bam, because M.J. is in the hospital while he's driving around with the motherfucka responsible like it was nothing. Then he asked me if I was scared that Drugs and 'em would try and do something to me. I told him 'Hell no!' I told him my people would make this whole neighborhood hotter than it is now. Drugs doesn't want any part of me."

"What did he say after that?" Chuck asked referring to Eric.

"Nothing," I responded. "That was it. Me and Roberto left after that."

"Where are you?" Chuck asked.

"I'm at Calvin's house. Roberto's here too. When are you coming through?"

"I don't know yet. I'm still setting things up first."

"Good," I said. "I want to call Rodney and give him a time to come out here but I still don't know what Trip is doing later. I'm going to call Rodney anyway and see if he's still coming out here. Do me a favor? Call Carla and ask her what time she's coming out here."

"Alright," Chuck responded. "What time do you want me to call her?"

"As soon as possible. I have to know as soon as possible."

"Alright," he said, "I'll call you back."

"Later," I said. Roberto and Cal were still playing Madden Football and were seriously into the game. So, I decided to call Soraya first and find out how she and M.J. were. I called her cell but got her voicemail. She must've still been in the hospital. I left a message for her to call me back. I was restless and had a lot of things running around in my head. I wanted everything, in terms of the plan, to be over with already. Only because I didn't want to go back to the hospital and face M.J. without feeling that I'd done something to avenge his shooting. I didn't care and it didn't matter if I was right or wrong. I felt in my soul it was something I had to do. I called Rodney to find out whether he was still coming out.

"Rodney," I said. "You still coming out here?"

"Yeah, no question," he replied. "I'm waiting on a couple of my people. But I'm coming out there, no question. Are your people still watching that motherfucka?"

"Yeah," I replied. "We're just waiting on you now. Carla's coming out here too to see M.J. So if Trip sees her he's going to kick it to her. And I know you don't want that."

"Hell no, I don't want that. Yo, I'm definitely coming out there later on. I'm gonna call you when I'm on the way."

"Alright, later."

"What did he say?" Roberto asked prying his attention away from the video game for a moment.

"He's still coming out here," I responded. Now I just had to get the verification on what Trip was going to do that night.

Chapter 12

It had been hours and I was still waiting for a specific phone call. I had spoken to Soraya, my mom and Chuck. Soraya was at home and my mother was at the hospital with M.J. Soraya asked me if I was going to see M.J. I explained to her that I wanted to but I had to go ahead with what I was doing. I was so thirsty for revenge that I was tempted to just blast Drugs. I wanted to take his life for almost taking my son's life. The day before at the park, if the cops hadn't been on the way, I more than likely would have shot Drugs. A few minutes later and my life might have changed forever. My rage was at a boiling point when I came face to face with him.

Afterwards, I was glad that I didn't shoot him. If I had, I would've been away from my family for years, if not the rest of my life. There were risks with the plan. Not as big a risk as going out and shooting him myself but it was risky just the same. Soraya understood that I had to go through with it. She wanted something done just as much as I did. She actually wanted Drugs dead. Her feelings didn't waver in that respect. She just didn't want anything happening to me.

I could tell in her voice that she was as emotionally drained as was I. She didn't sound right. I hated her feeling the way that she did. I vowed to take care of my family with all my being but I felt like I failed them. That was probably what also fueled the craving I had to make everything right, or as right as it could possibly get.

I hadn't spoken to Brian in a while and that was on my mind also. I knew he needed me but I couldn't speak to him. I couldn't face him or M.J. He asked to speak to me but I told Soraya to tell him that I would speak to him later. It was fucked up of me but I just couldn't speak to him.

Soraya told me to be careful in doing the plan and I reassured her that I would. I told her that Carla was going to be at our house around 6:00 pm and that Chuck was going to drop her there. I told her how the plan was progressing. We gave each other our love and I told her I'd give her the status of everything later on that night.

It was 6:10 pm and I was so anxious that I was going out of my mind. I'd been pacing the whole day and was preoccupied.

"Malik," Roberto said. "Chill out. Everything's going to work out."

"I hope so," I responded. "As soon as I get this phone call, I'll feel better." About forty minutes later, I got the phone call I'd been waiting for and it was good news. Trip would be at Club Cocoa's that night. Now everything could proceed. I hung up and told Cal and Roberto the news.

"It's on fellas," I said. "Trip's going to be at Cocoa's tonight."

"Alright," Roberto said. "It's about time. I'm sick of kicking Cal's ass in this game."

"Fuck you," Cal responded. "You didn't kick my ass. You won seven games and I won six."

"Exactly," Roberto said. "I kicked your ass. Do the math. I won more games than you."

"Shut the hell up," Cal replied. As they went back and forth, I called Chuck and let him know that Trip was going to be at Cocoa's.

"Alright cool," Chuck responded. "Did you let Rodney know yet?"

"No, not yet," I replied. "I'm going to call him right after I get off the phone with you. Get all the fellas ready for tonight."

"They're ready," Chuck said. "Just let us know the time."

"You know how the plan is going to go, right?" I asked Chuck.

"Yeah. Don't worry. Everything is ready."

"Cool. I'll call you and let you know how it's going in a few."

"Alright."

"Is everything ready?" Roberto asked me after I hung up the phone.

"So far," I replied. "I'm calling Rodney right now."

I dialed his number as I checked the time on my watch.

"What's up?" Rodney asked me as I got him on the phone. "We're ready to come out there."

"I just got the confirmation that Trip is going to Cocoa's tonight," I responded. "Everything is set. Come out here now."

"Alright," Rodney said. "We're on the way."

"How many people are you coming out here with?" I asked.

"It's me and three others."

"OK, we'll go over everything again when you get out here," I said.

"Alright, later."

When I hung up from Rodney, it just hit me that I forgot to ask Chuck about Carla. Like I said, there was a lot of shit on my mind. I had to make sure that she was OK. I called my house and Carla answered.

"Carla, I'm just calling to make sure that you got there alright."

"Yeah. Chuck picked me up and told me what was up."

"Good," I said, "Rodney's on his way out here now. This shit's about to go down."

"Let us know what happens and be careful."

"Thanks, we will."

"We're about to go see M.J.," she told me. "Do you want to speak to Soraya before we leave?"

"No," I replied. "I already spoke to her. I'll speak to her again later." After I hung up, Roberto, Cal and I went over the plan again. Everything was understood and again we played the waiting game.

"Yo, we're outside your building," Rodney said as I answered my cell phone about an hour after we last spoke.

"We're not there," I told him. "We'll be there in five minutes. Wait in your car because we're leaving as soon as we get there." I told him that so he wouldn't try to go to my apartment. I didn't want to take any chances of conflict between him and Carla. More than likely Carla was at the hospital anyway.

Before I even hung up from Rodney, Roberto and Cal had their burners in their waistbands. We marched out of Cal's apartment with purpose. On the walk towards my building, I gave Roberto my phone and asked him to call Chuck to meet us in front of the building.

"He said he'll be there in about five minutes," Roberto said after speaking to Chuck.

"Good," I replied. We arrived around the way and as we walked towards Rodney's car, him and his boys stepped out. We gave pounds and introduced ourselves to each other.

I looked Rodney straight in his eyes and asked him, "Are you ready?"

"No doubt, let's do this," he responded.

"I'm waiting for my man Chuck," I said. "He'll be here in a few; then we'll go to Cocoa's. But before that, let me make this phone call."

"Alright," he said, "Is Carla upstairs?"

"She's at the hospital with Soraya," I told him. "Excuse me." I walked away, made the call and got the information that I needed. Chuck and Tyrell pulled up alongside me in Chuck's car.

"Ready?" Tyrell asked me.

"No question," I replied. "C'mon, let me introduce ya'll." We walked over to the group and I said, "Chuck, this is Rodney. Rodney, Chuck." They exchanged pounds and both Chuck and Tyrell met the rest of Rodney's crew.

"I just got the word that Trip is on his way to Cocoa's now," I told everyone. "So we should get going."

The large group hopped into the two cars and drove towards Club Cocoa's. The ride to the club was quiet. I attributed that to everyone getting mentally prepared. I put my head in my hands and took a deep breath. As I exhaled, it was as if all my problems and all that I was going through, left my body, leaving only a moment of clarity. It allowed me to think clearly about any and every aspect of the plan. Not that I hadn't thought about everything before, but this was different. It was like I knew that the plan would work because if there were any roadblocks or deviations, I would see them in my mind before they happened. I would know what to do to make it work. This is the best way I could explain it. With that clarity came, if only for a brief moment, a relaxed feeling.

I enjoyed it while I could because I knew it wouldn't last. As I looked out the window, I saw that we were getting closer to our destination. With each street, traffic light and group of people out enjoying the muggy summer night, I felt the calm feelings slowly draining out of me. No matter what I tried to think about or how many deep breaths I took, I couldn't recapture those calm feelings. I knew that there was no more talking about the plan. It was time to go through with it. It was finally going down.

I was extremely anxious. It's something only a parent could understand. It doesn't matter if someone has a hundred little cousins, nieces or nephews. If you don't have your own child, you'll never understand the feelings I had. The feelings of seeing your child hurt as well as the rage and need for vengeance that consumes you. My train of thought was broken by Chuck's car suddenly braking. My hands slammed against the dashboard. He stopped to avoid hitting a crackhead that was crossing the street against the light without even looking.

"Get the fuck out the street motherfucka!" Chuck yelled at the disheveled man. The crackhead didn't skip a beat. He didn't acknowledge almost getting run down in the street.

"When it's time to get high, those crackheads don't see shit but the crackhouse." Chuck proclaimed --still agitated by the jaywalker. I stayed quiet. I looked at my watch and it was still early. Usually when we go to Cocoa's we don't go until about one in the morning. That's when a lot of strippers that had other bookings showed up. So there was more of a variety, at the late hours, so to speak.

That night was different in that Cocoa's was having a 'Lock Door,' which is when you pay $20 and up for admission and the doors are locked by a certain time. No one gets in or out for hours, usually daybreak. Once inside, you can do anything with the strippers. Anything goes. There's food and alcohol of course but those are secondary. Plus, there was supposed to be some porno chick showing up so a large crowd was expected.

"We're about three blocks away," Chuck said. "Where are we going to park?"

"Pull over right there," I replied pointing to the corner of 221st Street. Chuck put his indicators on to let Rodney know that we were pulling over. We all stepped out of our cars.

"The club is a couple of blocks away." I said to Rodney. "Go two blocks straight down to that second stoplight and make a right. It's in the middle of that block. Look for a black Jaguar, that's Trip's car. Cal and Roberto are going to be lookouts on the next two blocks. Chuck and I are going be here. If Po-Po is coming, then we'll hit you on the cell and let you know before they get on the block. Now Trip is going to come running out of the club, once your boy sets things up. He's wearing a white New York Knicks jersey. He's also wearing a black baseball cap and jeans. You'll know it's him cause he's going to go straight to the Jaguar. Whatever ya'll are gonna do, it has to go down quickly. More than likely, he's not going to come out by himself. He's going to have his crew with him. This shit has to be done correctly so ya'll gotta be ready. Alright, let's go."

Chapter 13

"**I** see the black Jaguar," Rodney said to me as we spoke on the phone. He drove past Cocoa's to see how many people were outside the club and see where Trip's car was in relation to the front of the club.

"The Jag is parked about 20 feet away from the front of the club," Rodney said.

"Good," I replied. "Send your boy in now."

"Go ahead Dave," I heard Rodney say in the background to his man. Dave walked up the block, from the corner, to Cocoa's. He paid his admission and entered. They hadn't locked the club down yet so you could still go out of the club and reenter it. Security put a stamp on your hand to keep track of who paid. Whoever went into the club, in this case Dave, was to go directly to Trip and ask him if he drove a black Jaguar. When he confirmed that he did, he would tell Trip that someone was breaking into his car. Apparently, Dave told him because Trip came racing out of the club. He was followed by a few of his boys. From up the block, Rodney's car sped up towards Trip. Rodney was in the passenger seat, on the same side as the club, and his man was driving. Another dude was sitting behind Rodney.

The lights were turned off on the car so no one could see the license plate number. POP, POP, POP, POP, POP echoed in the night. We heard the barrage of gunfire from where Chuck and I were. I heard at least five but there could have been more. They sounded like firecrackers. We could pretty much tell what kind of gun was being fired, just by hearing it.

"That sounded like a .25," I said to Chuck. He just nodded his head. He had a look of trepidation on his face. He looked in both directions to see if Rodney's car was coming. Rodney would have to come back around to where we were because he didn't know how to get out of the neighborhood. Cal and Roberto came running back to Chucks' car.

"Yeah!" Cal said excitedly. "That's what I'm talking about."

"Chill with that," I told him. I didn't want attention being brought to us.

"They'd better hurry up," Roberto said about Rodney and his crew. He was right. We couldn't wait there all night with cops on the way. Then coming in our direction, on the opposite side of the street, was Rodney's car. They were speeding.

"Why the fuck are they driving like that?" Roberto asked rhetorically. "That's going to attract attention." Their car busted a U-turn with the tires screeching like they were in a movie. Chuck started driving off with Rodney behind us. We drove calmly for about five minutes before we pulled over.

We got out of our respective cars on a block filled with burned out and abandoned buildings.

"Why was ya'll driving like that?" I asked them.

"Yo, we had to get out of there," Rodney replied.

"What happened?" I asked.

"I went in and asked Trip if he drove a black Jaguar," Dave replied. "He said yes and I told him that his car was being broken into. He didn't even bother asking how I knew he drove a Jag. Once he heard about his car being broken into and possibly stolen, he jetted out followed by his crew. He said something to his boys as he was running out but I didn't hear what he said. I stayed inside the club until I heard the shots, then I ran out with everyone else."

"We saw him run to the Jag and we wet him," Rodney said. "Him and two other dudes that ran to the car with him. I guess they were his people. As soon as they got to the car, we started shooting. The two dudes that came out with him were running so hard to get to the Jag that when they saw that they were about to get wet, they slid trying to stop their momentum. They tried to run away but we got them. Trip was in front so we definitely got him. He was the first hit."

"How many times did you hit him?" Chuck asked Rodney.

"I don't know," Rodney replied. "A few times."

"Give me the burners and I'll get rid of them," I told them.

"Nah," his man responded. "For what?"

"If cops pull ya'll over, ya'll don't want these burners in your car," I replied. "And the way ya'll were driving after a shooting in front of a club, someone more than likely saw your car."

"I don't know," Rodney said.

"I'm looking out for ya'll." I told them. "If ya'll want to go to jail tonight then keep the shits in your car. But I strongly suggest that you let me take care of it. I told you I'd look out for ya'll and I will. But decide right now because Po-Po is on the way. If they see a car with more than one person, they're going to pull the car over. The highway is about two blocks away. Ya'll could just get on and be out. But let me know right now."

"Alright, alright," Rodney said, handing over the gun. I took it, looked at it and said, "Damn, a .25? Did ya'll at least break his skin with this?" I asked sarcastically.

"Yeah," Rodney replied like he was insulted by my question.

"What do you have?" I asked his man. He reluctantly handed me his gun. "Wow," I said looking at the small .22 caliber gun. "Alright, I'll take care of it. We gotta go. To get to the highway, make a left here at the corner, drive a couple of blocks down and you'll see the highway. I'm gonna call you later on and let ya'll know what's up. Alright, later." We got in our cars and drove off.

We got back around the way and dropped Cal and Roberto off. It was time to get off the streets and keep a low profile. Chuck and I got to the building. Chuck brought the guns to his apartment and we went our separate ways for the night. Soraya and Carla were at the hospital. More than likely they were spending the night there. I needed to speak to her and tell her all the shit that went on. I left a message on Soraya's voice mail to call me back. I didn't get into specifics. I still had a few more things to do the next day, so I showered and went to sleep.

The next morning, Soraya woke me up and said, "Chuck's on the phone." Usually I hear the phone ringing when I'm sleeping but I guess I hadn't caught up with my rest yet.

"How're you doing?" I asked her.

"I'm fine, just tired," she responded. And before I could ask she said, "M.J. is OK. He's still in pain but he's getting better. He's been asking for you. When are you going to see him?"

"Later on today."

"Brian's been asking for you too," she said. "I'm going to see them today. I still have shit to do. It ain't over yet. Where's Carla?"

"She went to work," she replied. "Here, talk to Chuck. We'll talk after."

"Sorry about that," I told Chuck.

"That's cool," he responded. "We have things to do. Get up."

"Yeah," I said. "Anything new?"

"Yeah actually," he replied. "First, Trip isn't dead."

"What?" I asked in amazement.

"You heard me," Chuck said. "He isn't dead. He only got hit twice. Once in his hand and once in the thigh."

"All them shots and he only got hit twice?" I asked.

"Yeah."

"What about the other dudes?"

"Nobody died," Chuck said.

"I can't believe that shit," I said in amazement. "Those motherfuckas can't shoot straight. They must've been real nervous. Plus they were using those little ass guns. A .22 and a .25 ain't gonna do shit to anyone."

"I know it," Chuck said.

"If those motherfuckas were using glocks, shit would've been different," I said. "They would've been taking permanent naps right now."

I kissed my teeth and said, "Shit." I couldn't front, deep down, I wanted him dead. I wanted Trip, Drugs and everyone, who was involved in M.J. getting shot, dead. And I was upset that Trip wasn't. A surge of anger overtook me.

"You mean after all this planning, this motherfucka is still walking around living?" I asked.

"And my son is still in the hospital because of their bullshit."

"Don't worry," Chuck said. "You know it isn't over. We still have more shit to do. So get up."

"Alright," I said kind of pissed.

"I'm gonna drop this shit off first," Chuck told me.

"Yeah," I said impatiently. I wanted to get off the phone because I was pissed. "I'll call you back," I said to him. I hung up the phone; sat at the edge of my bed and took a deep breath.

That shit had me fuckin' pissed. Regardless of what I told Rodney, I wanted him to shoot Trip and kill him. They harmed my kid and I wanted them harmed in return. But like Chuck said, it wasn't over. There was more to the plan than what happened at Cocoa's. I had to focus on that.

Soraya walked in the room, looked in my face and gave me a hug. At that moment, that's what I needed. She knows me well and knows what I need. There were no words exchanged between us. They weren't needed. I enjoyed the comfort and warmth of that hug. I had been missing that the last few days. Finally, I broke the silence by saying, "Trip isn't dead."

"I know," she replied. "Chuck told me everything that happened." I looked at her and said, "I have to finish this."

"I know," she responded. "Are you going to wait for me to get Brian so you can say hello?"

"No, I have to go right now," I replied. "I have to do this first. I don't want to face him until I finish this, and I'm going to finish it today."

"OK," she said. "Be careful though."

"I will." With that, I got up, got ready and left. I walked out of the building and the sun was shining brightly. It caused me to squint my eyes and contort my face. I wasn't in the mood for any shit. No one I cared to talk to was out, so I sat on the benches and chilled. After a while, I was so impatient that I decided to call Chuck. I couldn't wait for him to call me back. It had been an hour and change since I spoke to him last and I was hoping he had some news for me. I was restless. Then I said, "Fuck it" and decided to wait for him to call me. I got up and decided to go to the bodega to get some water.

"What's up Malik?" one of the neighborhood youngsters asked me. I didn't respond verbally. I nodded my head in acknowledgment and kept it moving. It was still relatively early but it was already hot as hell outside. While walking there, I saw some other people from around the way. I acknowledged them also but I wasn't in the mood for talking. I was approaching the bodega when my phone rang. At that exact same time, a car pulled up in front of the bodega. Drugs stepped out of that car with two other dudes. One of them was Bam. I stopped in my tracks. All three of them were walking into the store. They didn't see me at first. I felt something inside of me snap.

Everything, all the emotions, all the pain, came to the surface. At that moment, I felt pure rage. I walked straight towards them. First, Bam saw me and then the other dude that was with them. Then Drugs saw me. I went towards him. He's the one I wanted. As I was about to pounce on Drugs, Bam and the other dude grabbed and held my arms.

"What the fuck are you doing?" the other guy holding me asked angrily.

"Get the fuck off of me!" I yelled. "You can't fight me like a man? You need other motherfuckas to help you fight?" We were face to face and I was yelling all in his face. I was so worked up that spit was flying out of my mouth with damn near every word. I was spittin' venom.

"Fuck You!" Drugs yelled back at me. "Who the fuck are you? You ain't shit, motherfucka."

Pop came running out of the bodega and yelled, "Stop this shit right now!"

Drugs yelled back at him, "Shut the fuck up and get back in that fuckin' store before I knock you out!" 'Pops' took his ass right back in the bodega. I was struggling to get myself loose so I could knock Drugs out. Drugs at that time was taking his watch and chain off. While he was taking them off, he was also talking shit.

"I'm gonna fuck you up, you bitch ass motherfucka," he said. I guess he was trying to hype himself up.

"Fuck all that talk," I told him. "Tell these bitch ass motherfuckas to let me go and we'll see what's up."

"Shut the fuck up!" The other guy holding me said as he angrily tugged on my arm.

"Let him go," Drugs told them. Before they let me go, Drugs was already in motion of throwing a punch. It was a haymaker that caught me dead in my mouth. The punch knocked my bottom lip unto my teeth, opening up a gash.

"Yeah punk, what?!" Drugs yelled. As I spit blood onto the concrete, I knew I had to control my emotions enough to win this fight.

"C'mon motherfucka," I said as I put my hands up. I feigned a couple of right hands and he jumped back. I feigned another right and caught him with a left hook. He stumbled but stayed on his feet. He got pissed and I knew he was going to try and throw wildly to try and catch me right back. I turned my head slightly to the side to spit more blood out and he threw another wild punch. I knew he was going to throw it but he still caught me. He didn't catch me flush because at the last moment, I was able to turn my head enough so that he wouldn't. Drugs was fast with his hands but I was better. The last punch he threw caught me on that bone between my temple and jaw line. No big deal.

We were moving around and I was watching his chest. I saw his chest flex and that let me know he was going to throw another right punch. I easily got out of the way of that punch and countered with a right of my own that caught him on his forehead. It put a knot right above his left eye. He looked like he was dazed by the punch. So right away, I feigned another right and caught him with a left hook and followed with a right cross. That combination put him on his ass. I pounced on him and hit him as hard as I could. 'Boom!' was the sound the first punch made as it resonated in the air. It landed on his forehead. "That was for M.J. motherfucka," I said through clenched teeth. He was on his back trying to cover his face but it was no use. I was hitting him hard. My punches went through his weak defense. He couldn't stop it. 'Boom!' Another punch landed in his face.

"That was for putting my family through so much shit."

'Boom!' "That was for fuckin' up the neighborhood."

'Boom!' 'Boom!' I punched furiously and I swear I could have killed him. I was letting out all my frustrations and all the shit I'd endured because of that motherfucka.

"Don't you ever fuckin' harm anyone in my family." I said as I continued pounding him. Blood was pouring from his wounds and soaked my hands. I must have caught his teeth during my attack because my knuckles had cuts in them and were in pain.

I heard Drugs say, "You got it," in a low voice as if that would stop him getting beat down. 'Fuck that,' I thought to myself and continued punching harder. There was no way he was getting any mercy from me. It was like I was possessed. As I wailed away on him, someone grabbed me from behind. Before I could react, the sound of the fast police siren closed in.

Whoever grabbed me, let me go and started to run. Drugs was stunned but when he heard those sirens, he stumbled to his feet. His face was a mess. He was unrecognizable. He jumped up and got in his car quickly. Bam and that other guy moved towards the car but Drugs drove off. He left them. They called for him to wait so they could get in the car but Drugs wasn't trying to stop to let them in. He was all for self. They ran off cursing Drugs.

At that point, I started running. I knew 'Pops' called the cops and they would be there shortly. Once they saw me with a bloody lip, a knot on my face and swollen bloody hands, they would pick me up. I didn't full out sprint, I did more of a jog away from the scene. I heard that the police sirens were upon me but they bypassed me and converged on Drugs car in the middle of the street. He was surrounded. I guess 'Pops' told the cops about Drugs and described his car because they went right for him. While he was cornered, this dumb ass Drugs, tried to drive onto the sidewalk. But being that he was surrounded, his car crashed into a mailbox. Once his car came to a stop after hitting the mailbox, Po-Po opened his car door and pulled him out. They had their guns drawn. They had him face down on the concrete.

While Drugs was handcuffed, the cops started searching his car. One tall cop put on rubber gloves and leaned in the front of the driver's side. After a few seconds, he came out of the car holding two small caliber handguns. The same two guns that shot Trip the night before.

"That shit ain't mine!" yelled Drugs referring to the guns.

"Then how'd it get here?" the cop asked.

"Ya'll put that shit there," Drugs responded.

"Is this what you used to shoot Trip?" the cop asked sarcastically. "We have the slugs that were taken out of him. We're going to check the ballistics on those slugs and these guns. If they match, you're fucked."

"Those are not my fuckin' guns," Drugs said again. "Ya'll are trying to frame me. My fingerprints ain't on them guns. Check 'em." Drugs kept yelling, "Those ain't my guns."

"That's why you were trying to get away so quickly, right?" the cop asked.

"This is some bullshit!" Drugs said as they picked him up and put him in one of the patrol cars.

"This is some bullshit!" he repeated over and over.

Chapter 14

After changing my blood-stained shirt and applying ice to my busted lip, I went to my parent's house to see Brian. No one was there. I went back home and got my car keys and headed to the hospital. Coming off the elevator and walking towards M.J.'s hospital room, I felt relieved that I'd done something. I could feel people looking at my swollen, cut lip. I didn't care though. I kept walking with purpose to the room never directly looking at anyone or acknowledging their looks. To me, my lip was a battle scar of which I was proud. I walked into M.J.'s room and the saw the whole family. My parents, Soraya and Brian were all there. Carla was probably at her house.

"What happened to your lip?" my father asked as I gave hugs and kisses to everyone. "And your swollen hands?"

"Long story," I replied. "I'll explain later. Come here Brian." He seemed reluctant to come to me. The reality of seeing his brother like that probably had more to do with it than anything else.

"He's been like that since we got here," Soraya told me.

"Brian," I said again, "Come here." He slowly walked to me and as I bent down, he gave me a sincere, heart filled hug that brought tears to my eyes. "Listen," I said carefully choosing my words, "M.J. is going to be alright. He's going to stay here for a little while so that the doctor can help him get better. Then he'll be home with us and you two will be playing again. You don't have to feel sad because he'll be OK and I'm going to make sure that nothing happens to you or M.J. Daddy is going to take care of ya'll. OK?" He nodded his head.

"Daddy?" M.J. asked in an almost whispered voice.

"I'm here," I said as I walked over to him and leaned over to look him in the face. Brian came over to M.J. also and held his hand. "What happened to your mouth?" M.J. asked.

"It's nothing," I replied. "How are you doing?"

"I'm OK Daddy," he replied. "I want to go home."

"Not yet," I told him. "The doctor is going to make you better first and then you'll come home. But you have to be strong. Can you be strong?"

"I want to go home Daddy," M.J. said with tears coming down his face and in a voice that would break anyone's heart.

As Brian wiped M.J.'s tears, I said, "I know you want to go home but you have to stay here for just a little while longer so you can get better." At that point, tears were streaming down my face as well. "You'll be home soon and someone will always be here with you until you do come home. Please understand, we don't want to keep you here, but you do want to come home and play with Brian, don't you?"

"Yes," he said. "That's why you have to stay here while you get better. Alright?"

"OK," he said. I wiped away his tears as well as my own. Damn, I wished I could have taken him home with us.

"I love you this much Daddy." M.J. told me as he tried to spread his arms apart. He couldn't spread them wide because he had tubes in him and was weak from his injuries. But to me, him doing that was worth everything that I had done.

"I love you this much too," I responded as I spread my arms wide.

"Daddy?" he asked.

"Yes?"

"Did you get the bad men that shot me?"

"Yeah," I replied, "I got them."

Cut to the present. It's now October and I'm currently sitting here in the Brooklyn Supreme Court. It's been a few months since Drugs was arrested and I'm here as a spectator at his trial. He has numerous charges that include attempted murder and possession of a deadly weapon. He has multiple counts of each.

It didn't help Drugs that when the cops checked the ballistics of the two guns found in his car, they matched the slugs taken out of Trip. It also didn't help him that he was the only one in the car when he got caught. There was a fairly quick turnaround from Drugs arrest to the time of his trial. This was mainly because of the media attention this case attracted. Cops, prosecutors and the neighborhood, in which he dealt, knew he was a dealer.

But outside of that, the rest of the city and state had no idea who Drugs was, at first. The story was only picked up locally in the beginning. It received wider coverage when it was found that he had the whole neighborhood terrorized. With the stories of shootings, beatings and various acts of unlawfulness, the mainstream media couldn't get enough. Especially when they thought that Drugs shot his right hand man, Trip, because he found out that Trip was screwing his girl. It became a media frenzy, from local story to front page of the Daily News. Reporters from the TV news channels converged on Woodson and the Plaza. They asked residents numerous and repetitive questions. They wanted to know everything about Drugs and how bad he made the neighborhood. The media was trying to play up the urban ghetto violence angle but that was nothing new. There were news vans double-parked all over the place. The amount of attention this case received was ridiculous.

The prosecutors pushed for this case to go to trial quickly because they were embarrassed that they hadn't been able to convict Drugs for anything for a significant amount of time. When the media found that out, the prosecution looked, for lack of a better word, inept. Especially since a lot of people got shot because of Drugs, including M.J.

Speaking of M.J., he's back home with us and doing well, as well as could be expected. He's running around and seems happy. Both he and Brian are showing no apparent effects of the shooting incident. Aside from occasional nightmares by M.J., he seems OK. We don't know what, if any, long-term effects may be. We'll just have to keep watching them and hope for the best.

As the jury came back from deliberation, we anxiously awaited the verdict. They'd only been away a couple of hours and we didn't know what to make of that short amount of time. The tension in the courtroom was high. It seemed like everyone was there as spectators or tried to get in as spectators. There were police and people from the neighborhood there in unity for a common interest, at least on that day. The judge asked the foreperson if the jury had come to a verdict on the attempted murder charge.

"Guilty," she said. The courtroom erupted. People clapped, the media ran out of the courtroom to report on the verdicts and people let out sighs of relief. I was sitting behind Drugs so I couldn't see his face or tell his reaction. I wanted to look in his eyes but he never turned around. Even when people in court yelled things at him, he never acknowledged the comments. The judge had to tell everyone to be quiet. When order was restored, the verdicts for the other charges were read. All the major charges were guilty. Drugs was remanded back to Riker's Island.

He got up and was taken away, never turning his head. I was satisfied in that I knew he was going to be incarcerated for years. But I also knew that no matter how many years they gave him, it would never be enough. I wasn't satisfied that nothing happened to Trip. I know he got shot but he's still living. He didn't go to jail and wasn't charged with anything. That's the bad news. The good news is with Drugs conviction, his reign of terror is over. His crew is finished.

I heard that Trip was somewhere down south. Good riddance to him. Yvette is going out with some new guy from Woodson. I'd heard he was in the music industry but I don't know how true that is.

Mack was buried shortly after his family took him off of life support. His brother, Rick, is back around the way. He's doing OK.

I haven't heard about anyone seeing Lou since they shot at him. The rumor is that he's living with his sister in Jersey.

We never did find the teens that shot at Lou and actually shot M.J. But sooner or later we'll find out who they were and get them. There was an increased and constant police presence in the neighborhood following Drugs' arrest. With Drugs conviction, the cops didn't want anyone replacing his operation. The neighborhood is safer now and there hasn't been the violence like before. There's still tension between dudes from the Plaza and Woodson but not like it was before. It's an uneasy truce but people from both sides are talking about starting the basketball tournaments again next summer. We'll see how that goes.

Believe it or not, after all the drama they've been through, Carla is still with Rodney. I can't understand it but if she wants to stay with him that's her business. I haven't heard about any recent fights between them so hopefully shit is better between them. He calls me trying to talk and hang out. I don't want to hang out with him. I ain't cool with him like that. I just give him excuses. He thanks me for looking out for him and getting rid of the guns. I never told him how I got rid of them. He just knows that they're gone and he can't get them back.

Right before I fought Drugs outside the bodega, I got a phone call that I didn't answer. I later found out that it was Chuck. He was calling to tell me that the guns were placed in Drugs' car. That was part of the plan. I used Rodney's ego and temper to have him do something to Trip. Then I had the guns put in Drugs car. The cops would have found the guns in Drugs car and it would be a wrap. Like I said, everything almost worked. It's not over.

If I ever see Trip again, I'm going to finish it. I walked out of the courthouse and into the chilly afternoon. With everything that's gone on circling in my mind, I heard a familiar voice call out to me.

"Yo, Malik." I turned around, walked towards him and gave him a pound.

"What's going on?" I asked. But before giving him a chance to answer, I said, "Yo, thanks for everything. I couldn't have done all of this without your help." And it was true. He gave us information on Drugs and Trip, including Drugs cell phone number. But most importantly, he stashed the guns in Drugs car. The plan wouldn't have gone as well as it did if not for him.

"No problem," he responded. "I would hope you would do the same for me."

"No question," I replied. "I really appreciate what you did."

"You got it," he replied.

"You going back around the way now?"

"No, I got some things to do first," he responded. "I just came down here to try and get in the court but it was packed up in there."

"Yeah, it was."

"Yo," he said, "We'll get up later."

"No doubt," I told him as we gave each other pounds again. "Alright, take it easy Bam." With that, we walked in different directions. Only this time, all the bullshit is dead and we're cool again. Why would Bam help me in the first place if we had beef? I called him after M.J. got shot, told him about my plan and asked for his help. He told me something that I'll always remember. He said, "I have a son that I love also and I'll do anything for him."

Chapter 15

"It's freezing out here," Roberto said to me as we walked towards Macy's on Fulton Street.

"Hell yeah," I responded. "And it's crowded as fuck out here."

"What do you expect?" Roberto asked me. It was two days before Christmas and people were braving the cold temperatures and crowds, to complete their shopping lists, or in our case, we were just beginning.

"Do you know what you're getting Soraya?" Roberto asked me.

"Yeah. She wants this diamond bracelet that she saw at Macy's. It's expensive, but it's on sale right now. I hope they're not sold out."

"Soraya knows that you're getting her that?" he asked.

"Yeah. She asked me to get it for her. She's hard to shop for, so I just ask her what she wants and she tells me."

"Alright," Roberto replied. We arrived at Macy's and walked through the doors. We walked out of the bleeding cold and into the oppressive heat. It felt like a sauna. It was ridiculous. I took off my coat and held it under my arm.

"Look at that shit," Roberto said referring to the sea of people below as we ascended the escalator. People were pushing, arguing, and yelling. Roberto and I saw two women fighting over the last stuffed Elmo doll. They were actually fist fighting over a stuffed doll. Four security guards were trying to pry them apart. It was crazy in there. Christmas in Brooklyn, I love it. We arrived at the jewelry section on the

2nd floor and I asked the sales associate if there were any more bracelets.

"Let me check for you," she responded.

"You'd better hope they're not sold out, or you're in trouble," Roberto said.

"You're right about that," I replied. "I still have to get my parents something also. I don't know what the fuck I'm going to get them. It's a good thing that Soraya is getting the presents for M.J. and Brian."

"Here you go," the sales associate said to me as she handed me the bracelet.

"Thank you."

"That's hot," Roberto said to me. "Soraya's going to like it."

"Yeah," I replied. As I looked at the bracelet, something caught my attention at the corner of my eye.

"Oh shit!" I exclaimed.

"What?" Roberto asked me.

"C'mon," I said to him. I gave the bracelet back to the sales associate and hurried off.

"What is it?" Roberto asked.

"I just saw one of the guys that shot M.J."

"Are you sure? It's been over a year since that happened."

"It's him," I responded. "I'll never forget their faces. It was one of them. I'm sure of it."

"Where did he go?"

"I think he went towards the escalators," I told Roberto. "He was with two other dudes."

"Was both of the dudes that shot M.J. there?" he asked. "I don't know. I didn't see their faces. But I definitely recognized one of them." We pushed through the crowd of holiday shoppers. I didn't want to let him get away a second time.

"We gotta find him," I said. We frantically searched for him as we wiped away the sweat from our foreheads.

"Let's check outside," Roberto said to me. We walked back out into the bitter cold and it felt like the sweat from our faces would freeze instantly. We walked up and down Fulton Mall, which is an outdoor mall, looking for them but to no avail. They were nowhere to be found.

"Maybe they're still in Macy's," I told Roberto.

"Let's go check," he replied. We must have walked around the whole store three times.

"Shit!" I exclaimed. "I can't believe that motherfucka got away again."

"We'll get him eventually," Roberto responded.

"He was here," I said with more urgency. "I saw him and he got away again. I can't believe that shit!" All Roberto could do was reiterate that we would get the two guys that shot M.J. as well as Trip. But I knew there was no guarantee that I would ever see any of them again. It was almost a year and a half since M.J. was shot but time didn't heal the wounds. I was still thirsty for revenge. I had to get revenge. Unfortunately, I had a feeling that I would never see any of them ever again.

"Are you still going to get the bracelet?" Roberto asked me.

"Yeah." I was still looking around to see if I saw him. Roberto was trying to calm me down as I was standing there visibly fuming. Strangers were walking past me in all directions. Some people were looking to see why I was so upset.

"C'mon, let's go get that bracelet," Roberto said. We went back up to the jewelry section and purchased Soraya's present. "Are you getting anything for your parents now?" Roberto asked me.

"I may just give them money. I don't feel like shopping anymore. Let's just go back around the way. I don't feel like being around here."

"I here you," he responded. Before we left to go back to the Plaza, Roberto bought a few things to complete his Christmas shopping. My car was parked on a meter on one of the side streets. As we walked towards the car, I thought about the past two hours that we spent searching for that dude that shot M.J. I was quiet.

"Oh shit!" I exclaimed.

"What?" Roberto asked anxiously.

"There he is." I pointed to the teen walking in our direction with his friends. He was talking and laughing, oblivious to what I wanted to do to him at that moment. "I'm gonna kill him," I said through clenched teeth.

"No," Roberto said to me as he grabbed my arm to keep me from going after the teen.

"Get the fuck off of me," I said to him almost in a whisper. "No, let's just follow him."

"Fuck that."

"Listen," he said sternly. "You're not thinking. If you step to him now, you may never get the other dude that shot M.J. much less Trip. We want to get all those motherfuckas. Let's just follow him and see where he goes. Calm down. If we do shit correctly, we'll get all of those motherfuckas."

I heard Roberto out and reluctantly agreed. I knew he was correct in his thinking but I was just too angry to think logically at that time. It's a good thing he talked me out of doing something stupid. We watched them walk right past us and it took everything in my power not to punch the shit out of him. They didn't notice us. After they passed us, we stopped, turned around, and walked behind them. They were being loud as they walked down Fulton Mall.

We kept our distance from them, about fifteen to twenty feet away. I don't think they would've noticed us following them anyway. They were too into whatever bullshit they were talking about. One of the teens was talking on a cell phone and all three of them stopped on the corner of Jay Street. A shiny white Escalade screeched to a stop in front of them. When the teen that shot M.J. opened the door to the passenger side, I was shocked by what I saw.

"It's 'Trip,'" I said to Roberto.

"Yeah," he responded. "I told you. If we would've fucked them dudes up earlier, we wouldn't have seen Trip right now." I nodded my head as I continued staring at them enter the truck.

"Write down his license plate number," I said to Roberto. He walked to where he could see the back of the truck and not be seen. I just kept staring at them until they closed the doors. I didn't care if they saw me. I know that they didn't though. The truck then sped off and Roberto walked back to where I was standing.

"Did you get it?" I asked him. He handed the paper with the license plate number to me. "Are you sure this is it?" I asked.

"That's it," he responded. "Are you going to give it to that dude from your job?"

"You know it." He was referring to one of my co-workers, Curtis, whose brother works at the D.M.V. His brother can get information on anyone if we give him the license plate number or social security number. We would also have to give him $200 to do it. That's a small price to pay to get Trip and his people.

"I'm going to speak to him tomorrow," I said. "Let's get out of here." We went to my car and headed back to the Plaza.

Chapter 16

Fast forward to the next day at work, I spoke to Curtis and gave him the license plate number. I told him that I needed the information that day. It was Christmas Eve and I didn't want to wait to get the information after the holiday. "I'll call him during my break," Curtis said to me. "It's $200 for him to get that information though."

"I know," I replied. "I have the money right here." I gave him the money and the license plate number.

"I'll let you know what he says after I speak to him." Curtis told me. I didn't see him again till the end of our shift. I waited anxiously the whole damn day.

"Malik," he called out.

"What's up?" I asked him. "You have that information for me?"

"Of course," he responded. He handed me a piece of paper with the information I wanted.

"Thanks," I told him as I gave him a pound and walked away.

I think he wished me a Happy Holiday, but I wasn't really paying attention to him at that point. I looked at the information on the paper. The Escalade was registered to Yvette Hall, the same Yvette that used to fuck with Trip. The truck was registered in her name and address. It looked like she never stopped fuckin' around with him as everyone thought. I guess the rumor of her going out with that music industry dude was false. Therefore, she knows where Trip rests his head. That was good. Unfortunately, we couldn't just walk up to her and ask about Trip. If she were still with him, then there would be no way that she would give us any information on him. She would also warn him about us looking for him.

I sat down in the employee lounge and thought of what I could do with the information that I was blessed with. I must have been there for 45 minutes before it came to me. Then it all made sense.

I left work and when I got to the Plaza, I asked Roberto, Chuck, and Bam to come to my apartment. I spoke to them about what I wanted to do. M.J. and Brian were at my mother's house. All five of us, Soraya included, brainstormed and made alterations to my plan. We went over everything for about two hours.

"Are you sure you can get in contact with him?" I asked Bam.

"Yeah, no question," he replied. "I spoke to him two months ago. He wants Trip and them just as badly as you do. I would call him right now but I left his number at my house. I'll call him tonight and let him know what's up."

"Alright," I said to everyone. "Do we all understand what we're going to do?"

Chuck asked me a question and Soraya gave me another suggestion. We bounced more ideas back and forth and more questions were asked and answered. Finally, the plan was set. Because of that and since it was Christmas Eve, we poured out champagne.

I stood up, lifted my glass to the air and said, "I want to thank all of you for helping Soraya and I through this. You have no idea how much I love ya'll and I hope you know that I would do anything for ya'll. Merry Christmas." After the toast, Soraya and I picked up the kids and chilled for the rest of the night.

Two days after our meeting, I got a call from Bam.

"Malik, I spoke to him," he said. "He's with it. I knew he would be. I told him everything and he's ready. He gave me his cell number and told me to call him when it's time."

"Cool," I responded.

"Have you heard anything yet?" Bam asked me.

"Nothing yet," I replied.

"I'm about to go to Yvette's to start my shift of watching her."

"Alright then, just call me and let me know what's up."

"Yeah, I will," he replied.

"And good looking out for calling dude for me," I told Bam.

"No question. Later on."

"Later."

"I'm still here," Roberto said to me as we spoke on the phone. "Yvette's car is here. Still no movement." Roberto was parked on Yvette's block watching her house. "Let me know if she goes on the move." I said.

"Alright."

We hung up and I said to Soraya, "Roberto's still watching Yvette's house. Nothing yet." She nodded her head. Soraya and I had taken off from work. Chuck used some of his sick days, Bam used his vacation days and Roberto was in between jobs. We knew that Yvette would eventually lead us to Trip so we had people watching her house to see if Trip would show up. If he didn't show up at her house then she would go to him. We had to be patient at this point. We've waited all this time to get Trip, so waiting a little longer wouldn't hurt us. We knew that sooner or later that we would catch up to Trip. Roberto, Bam, Chuck and I took turns watching her movement. It had been three days since we've been following her. So far she's only been going shopping and hanging out with her girlfriends. We'll continue waiting and watching.

It was quiet in the house as the boys were again with my parents. I fell asleep. The phone rang and I hurriedly picked it up.

"Hello," I said. It was Roberto.

"Malik, I'm looking at the white Escalade right now."

"Where?" I asked excitedly.

"Bridgeport, Connecticut," he replied. "Yvette led me right to a townhouse with the Escalade in front of it. It's the same license plate number. She parked her car and went inside. She's been in there five minutes already."

"That's good," I said. "Soraya and I are gonna get ready. I'm gonna call Chuck and Bam and we'll be on the way."

"What about dude?" he asked.

"I don't have his number," I responded. "Only Bam has it, so he'll speak to him. How do I get up there?"

"Take I-95 straight up to exit 22," he responded. "When you get off that exit, go straight and at the second stoplight, make a left. Go straight to York Lane and make a right. Look for 3255. It's a beige townhouse. You'll see the Escalade right in front of it. Ya'll need to hurry up and get out here. It's going to take ya'll about an hour to get here. It's not that far from the Bronx. But I don't know how long Trip and Yvette will be here."

"It doesn't even matter if they stay there or not," I responded. "We know where he lives now so that's all we needed."

"Alright, get out here," he said.

"We're on the way, later." Soraya was in the room with me and when I hung up the phone she asked, "Did Roberto find them?"

"Yeah," I replied.

"All of them?"

"I don't even know. All he said was that both Trip and Yvette's cars were there. I don't know if those teenagers are there. I don't know who else is there. But we have to go now. It's going to take us a while to get up there."

While I was talking to Soraya, I hurriedly changed my clothes. Soraya was already dressed.

"Do you need me to call Chuck and Bam?" she asked.

"Call Chuck for me please," I replied. "I'm gonna call Bam myself.

"Alright."

She walked out of the room to make the phone call to Chuck. "It's time," I said to Bam as he answered his phone.

"It's about time. Where is he?"

"Bridgeport, Connecticut," I replied. "We're getting ready to go up there now. It's gonna take us about an hour to get there."

"I'm ready," Bam said to me. "I'm gonna call dude right now, don't worry." Bam knew that was going to be my next question and he answered it before I could ask.

"Good," I said. "I'm gonna get the car and I'll be at the front of the building. We have to hurry though."

"OK, let me call him now and I'll meet you outside," he told me. We hung up and I walked out to where Soraya was. She was still talking to Chuck. She told him that we were getting ready to leave. Chuck must have asked her a question because she was quiet for a moment then looked at me and asked, "Where are we going?"

"Connecticut," I responded.

"Connecticut," she said to Chuck. "Alright, bye." She hung up the phone and said, "Chuck said he'll be outside."

"Same with Bam," I told her. "Let's go baby."

With that, we left. All that was on my mind was that I hoped that I would finally have the complete revenge that I craved.

Chapter 17

I was nervous. I was extremely nervous actually. This was different than when Rodney shot Trip. This time I was going to be in the thick of shit. Not just myself though, Soraya was going also. On one hand, I would rather she not go. On the other hand, I'm glad she's down with me for whatever. She insisted on being a part of the plan. For what we'll be transporting in my car, it would be better if the cops see a couple in the car. Hopefully, we would be less likely to get pulled over. But that's not saying much because we can still get pulled over.

I'm also nervous because I'm not a teenager anymore. What I mean is I have more responsibilities now. I have a lot more to lose.

What we are about to do, does not have me worried to the point of calling it off though. It's just another problem that I have to take care of. I had a strong feeling though that our lives were going to change.

I was leaning on my car as Soraya sat inside being warmed by the heat. I was staring straight ahead, thinking about everything, oblivious to the cold. I don't know exactly how long I was waiting out there but it had to be about 20 minutes. Soraya tapped on the windshield, to alert me of Chuck driving in our direction on the opposite side of the street. He did a U-turn and double-parked in front of my car.

"How long have you been out here?" Chuck asked me as he waved hello to Soraya.

"It's going on half an hour."

"Have you spoken to Bam yet?" he asked.

"I'm still waiting on him."

"Shit, I hope Bam gets in contact with him," he said. "Have you spoken to Roberto yet?"

"No, I haven't spoken to him either," I responded. "I want to hear something soon though."

"How's M.J. and Brian?" he asked.

"They're good. They're with my parents again."

"Damn, they're always over there!" he joked. "You might as well give them custody."

Based on the bad vibes I was having about that night, I wasn't feeling that comment at all. I looked at him and only half jokingly said, "They're the grandparents, motherfucka. Are we supposed to keep them in the apartment by themselves?"

Sensing that I was cranky, he said, "Whoa, I'm just playing. Don't get excited. Everything is cool." It wasn't his fault that I was tense. I should have had more of a relaxed attitude like him.

"I'm cool," I said to him as I extended my hand to give him a pound.

"You gotta relax," he told me. "This is nothing new to us. We got this. This is our night."

"I hear you," I told Chuck. Him saying that didn't alleviate the bad vibes I had, but I had to keep it moving. Chuck and I were talking for 15 more minutes while Soraya stayed warm in the car. I hoped I had more gas in the car because she stayed in there with the engine running the whole time we were outside. I was impatient and growing more so every minute.

"What the fuck man?" I asked in frustration. "What's taking them so long?"

"Call them then," Chuck replied. I pulled out my cell and dialed Bam. The phone rang four times and went to his voicemail.

"Shit," I exclaimed. I redialed the number and got his voicemail again. This time I left a message. "We're waiting out here for you. Call me back." Chuck gave me a look that summed up how I felt at that moment. What I felt was total frustration.

Soraya rolled down the window and said, "I'm going to wait upstairs until they show up." She told me that before but I convinced her to stay.

My phone rang and I, in turn, said to Soraya, "This is probably one of them now."

"Hello," I said as I picked up the phone.

"Yeah, sorry it took so long," Bam said to me. "After I spoke to you, I called him and picked him up. Luckily, he was here in Brooklyn when I got in contact with him."

"Let me speak to him," I told him.

"Hello."

"What's up Lou?" I asked. "Where the fuck you been?"

"I'm maintaining," Lou replied. "I've been on the low, doing my thing. What's been going on with you? How's wifey and the kids?"

"They're good. Soraya's here with me right now. You'll see her when we meet up. M.J. is better."

"That's the one that got shot, right?"

"Yeah. He has a big ass scar in his stomach. Every time that I see it, I get pissed off."

"We're gonna to get those bitch ass motherfuckas," he said. "I owe them for killing Mack and trying to do the same to me. And for what they did to Rick. I let those motherfuckas sleep for a long time. Now it's time for payback."

"You're right about that," I said. "I appreciate you helping us out with this."

"Like I told you, I owe them. I got the shit you wanted me to bring."

"Good," I replied. "I got the money for it."

"You know what?" Lou asked. "Just give me half the money. I'll eat the other half. I've wanted to get them back for a while. I want revenge just as bad as you."

I found it strange that he only wanted to take half of the money. The first thing that came to my mind was that he had his own agenda. That's something that we didn't need.

But I accepted his offer of paying only half the money. I'm not stupid.

"Good looking out," I told him. "Where are ya'll?"

"We're on the way there," he told me. "Right now we're in Flatbush."

"Alright, we're going to get going," I said. I'll see ya'll there. Let me speak to Bam."

"Yeah," Bam said as he got back on the phone.

"Write this down," I told him. "It's the directions to where Trip is. You're going to have to meet us up there because we're leaving now."

I told Bam the directions and address and told him, "Ya'll gotta hurry up and get there. Roberto is up there watching the house now. But I don't know how long Trip and Yvette are going to be there."

"We're on the way," Bam said.

We hung up and I said to Chuck, "Let's go. Park your car and drive with us." He drove off as I got in my car. I told Soraya about everything that was said.

"It's about time," she said.

We drove up the block in the direction of the garage. Two minutes later, Chuck jogged out of the garage towards our car. I looked at him and nodded my head as if to say, "Let's do this." He nodded back, got in the car and we sped off.

We sped down the highway, swerving in and out of traffic. "Take it easy," Soraya said. "Get us there in one piece."

"Don't worry," I replied as I focused on the road. "Call Roberto and find out what's going on please."

"Who?" Soraya asked.

"Either one of you," I replied.

"I'll do it," Chuck announced.

After a couple of moments he said, "Roberto, we're on the way there now. We're on the highway."

"OK," he responded. "They're still inside the house. Ya'll better hurry up. Are Bam and Lou with you?

"No, we left before them."

"Damn," he said. You should have come together. That's just holding everything up. Like I said, I don't know how long they're going to stay here."

"It couldn't be avoided," Chuck told him. "Look, Bam had to pick Lou up. Now they're on the way up there and so are we. Don't worry. Shit's gonna be alright. We'll see you when we get there. Later."

I continued to fly up the highway at what could be considered excessive speeds. I didn't care if cops were on the highway. I should have been concerned about being pulled over, but I wasn't. I wanted to get up there. My baby, Soraya, didn't seem to mind at that point. I glanced over at her and she looked as focused as I was. I looked at the sign on the highway. We were already at Exit 15. I applied more pressure to the pedal and pushed the car to an even faster speed. The music was pumping loud out of the speakers and all of us were quiet. Chuck was bobbing his head to the infectious Timbaland beat that reverberated inside the car. There wasn't any deviation from that routine for the next couple of exits. My phone rang and I handed it to Soraya to answer it.

"Hello."

"Soraya, they're on the move," Roberto told her. "They just left the house. I'm following them now. They're driving the Escalade."

"Who's in the Escalade?" she asked.

"Just Trip and Yvette. The thing is, I don't know who else, if anyone, is in the house."

"We're almost there. We'll call you."

"Alright," Roberto replied.

Soraya closed the phone, handed it back to me and said, "Yvette and Trip left the house and Roberto is following them. He doesn't know if anyone else is in the house." I nodded my head and looked up at the sign. Exit 21. We were almost there, finally. I was relaxed enough at that point to bop my head to the music. Before I knew it, we were there. I looked up and the sign read, Exit 22, next right.

Chapter 18

Soraya was reading me the directions to Trip's townhouse. It didn't take long for us to find York Lane. Roberto's directions were perfect. We drove slowly up the block, looking at both sides, for 3255. The houses were well kept along this tree-lined street. It seemed like a quiet, safe place to raise your kids. A person would have to be pretty well off to have a house in this neighborhood. For Trip to have a townhouse here and a luxury SUV, only confirmed what we already assumed. He was still hustling. For as long as I've known Trip, I don't remember him ever having a "legit" job. He couldn't get the Escalade in his name because he has no job. The truck was paid for with his drug money, but he let Yvette, go buy it. The title and insurance must be in her name. I wondered whose name was on the lease for the townhouse.

Chuck spotted Yvette's Lexus and announced, "There it is. On the right side." I whipped my head in that direction and looked at Yvette's car. Then I looked at the two-story townhouse. Both floors had lights on. We briefly looked for any movement inside then we continued driving. We drove up the block, made a U-turn and parked. It was a safe enough distance where we could watch the house and not be seen.

"Make the call," I said to Soraya. She dialed 911 as I turned the music off and got quiet.

"Hello," she said. "Someone just stole my car. My name is Yvette Hall."

Soraya proceeded to tell them that she was Yvette and that a man, fitting Trip's description, carjacked her. She told them that it happened at Bridgeport Mall, which is very popular. Chuck and I sat there in amazement at the performance Soraya put on. If we didn't know any better, we would have believed that she was Yvette. She acted like she was crying and scared. She sounded real shook up. Soraya gave them the description and license plate number of Yvette's car. She answered whatever questions they asked her and she hung up from them.

"They said that they're going to dispatch some cars out," Soraya said to us.

"That was an excellent performance," I told her. "You did real good."

"Yeah, that was great acting," Chuck added.

"Thank you," she replied to our compliments. "So it was convincing?"

"Hell yeah," Chuck said.

"OK," she began. "They're going to send cops out looking for Yvette's car. So Bam and Lou just have to do their part now. I took out my phone and called Roberto.

"We're here," I said. "Where are they?"

"They're at Bridgeport Mall. They went into the movie theatre there. So it looks like you're going to have at least an hour and a half to do what ya'll gotta do."

"Good," I said. "I'm gonna find out where Bam and Lou are. If anything, call me back."

"Alright."

After informing Chuck and Soraya of the latest developments, I was about to call Bam. My phone rang. It was Roberto who immediately said, "Malik, They left the theatre. They may be on the way back to the house."

"Shit."

"What's wrong?" Soraya asked me.

"Yvette and Trip may be on the way back here."

"Damn," she said. "Is he sure?"

"Why do you think they're coming back here?" I asked Roberto. "They got back on the same highway that they took to get here. I'm not 100% sure that they are going back but it looks like they are. Maybe they changed their minds about the movie or the movie they wanted to see started at a different time. I don't know. I do know that ya'll gotta do that shit before they get there."

"How far is it from there to here?" I asked him.

"Maybe 20 minutes. It's not that far. Have you spoken to Bam yet?"

"I was just about to when you called."

"Call him now."

"Yeah. Later."

"How long do we have before Trip gets back here?" Soraya asked me.

"If they come straight here, about 20 minutes."

I called Bam and the first thing he said to me when he answered was, "We just passed exit 19. We're practically flooring it. We'll be there soon."

"Listen," I said. "They're not here right now so it's a perfect time to do this shit. But they're on the way back. They're about 15 minutes away."

"We're going as fast as we can."

"I need you to go faster," I said.

"Alright," he replied in a slightly agitated tone. "I'll call you back."

"Yeah."

"What did he say?" Chuck asked.

"He said he's driving as fast as he can to get here," I responded.

The only thing we could do at that point was wait and hope that Bam got here before Trip. If Trip got there first, the whole plan might be fucked up. Anxious minutes passed slowly. I was sweating so much that I had to crack the window. "Ya'll ain't hot?" I asked.

"No, I'm not hot," Soraya stated with attitude. "Please close the window." I closed it. The phone rang and it was Roberto.

"Malik," he said. "They are going back to the house. They're about 10 minutes away. Tell me that Bam is already there."

"No, he's not here but I'm gonna call him again right now."

"Fuck," he exclaimed. "It looks like everything is dead for today then."

"I'm gonna call him now," I told him with more emphasis. "I'll call you back. No, wait. Chuck call Bam on your phone." Chuck did it.

"I got him," Chuck said to me as Bam answered his phone. Then he asked Bam, "How far away are you?"

"We're just getting off exit 22," he replied. "We'll be there in a few."

"They're just getting off exit 22," Chuck announced to us.

"How close are they?" I asked Roberto.

"We're almost there." he replied. "What are ya'll gonna do?"

"Hold on," I told him and asked Chuck. "Where's Bam now?" Chuck asked Bam where he was and Chuck said to me, "They're looking for York Lane now."

"Tell them to hurry," I said.

"They're almost on the block," Roberto said. "They're only a few blocks away."

"Tell Bam to hurry the fuck up," I said to Chuck with more urgency.

"Ya'll have to get here now," Chuck said to Bam.

"We're here," he replied.

Chuck opened the window, looked out and said, "There they are."

"Who?" I asked as Soraya and I looked to see whom he was talking about. Then we saw Bam's Honda Accord driving in our direction. The car stopped in front of Trip's townhouse and Lou got out. He went over to Yvette's car, on the passenger side and kneeled out of sight. We knew what he was doing. The only problem now was that he had to do, what he was doing, before Trip got back.

"Bam is here," I told Roberto. "Yvette and Trip are at a stoplight two blocks from the house," Roberto told me. The light just turned green and they're almost on the block."

"Trip's almost here," I said to Chuck and Soraya.

"C'mon," Chuck said to Bam while staring at Yvette's car. Bam had his car right next to hers. If Trip came at that moment, he would see them.

"They're here," I announced as the Escalade turned onto the block. Just then, Lou darted back to Bam's car. He jumped in the car and they sped up the block in our direction.

"Done," Bam said to me.

"Good," I replied. "Later."

I hung up the phone with Roberto. Soraya, Chuck and I watched Trip and Yvette get out of the Escalade after parking. They walked in the house seemingly oblivious to what we had just done. Yvette glanced at her car but proceeded into the house.

"That's what I'm talking about," Chuck said to us. "No problem."

"Yeah right," Soraya said as she chuckled. We all knew that it was too close for comfort.

Finally, a lighthearted moment and a collective sigh of relief. I looked straight ahead and said, "Oh shit." I pointed to a figure, running in the middle of the street towards Trip's house. It was Lou. "What the fuck is he doing?" I asked rhetorically.

"I don't know what the fuck he's doing," Chuck answered. "He has something in his hand."

Sure enough he did as I squinted my eyes to try and see what it was. We figured out what it was quickly enough. He got right next to Trip's truck and threw a brick right through the driver's side window. It sounded like a mini-explosion. Broken glass littered the ground under the window and glistened against the nearby fluorescent streetlight. The alarm on the truck went off and was extremely loud and incessant. Some people started looking out of their windows while others came outside their houses.

We were stunned. Mouths open wide, stunned. Bam wasn't with Lou at that time and I wondered where he was. Just as quickly as Lou threw the brick through the window, he just as quickly leaned in the truck and picked it back up. He then ran a few feet to Yvette's car and threw the brick through her driver's side window. Her car doesn't have an alarm although it has a security system that kills the ignition.

Lou started screaming, "Come out here motherfucka!" Needless to say, Trip and Yvette came jetting out of the house. Running out, closely behind them, was one of the teenagers that shot M.J. He was the same one I saw at Fulton Mall. Trip ran into the street and briefly looked at both windows broken out. He then looked at Lou and charged at him as Lou aggressively asked, "WHAT???"

They started fighting hard. All the anger and hatred they have for each other boiled over. They were punching and wrestling each other with seemingly no concern for the broken glass on the ground or the people watching. All the while Yvette was screaming and cursing. We couldn't hear exactly what she was screaming, but we knew it was about the broken car windows and encouragement for

Trip to fuck Lou up. It was a big commotion but none of the neighbors, who came outside initially, tried to break up the fight. For that matter, no neighbors tried to break it up. Some of them went back in their houses. No doubt to call the police.

The teenager jumped in and started fighting Lou. At that point, Roberto's car pulled up followed by Bam. They got out of their respective cars and started fighting Trip and the teen. Seeing this, Chuck and I jumped out of the car and ran up the block towards them. The police sirens started blaring. Chuck and I were halfway towards the fight but stopped in our tracks once we heard the sirens. Yvette looked right at us. Judging by the look on her face, she recognized us. The sirens came closer and Bam and Roberto jumped back into their cars. Chuck and I ran back to my car.

While running back, I heard Bam yell for Lou to get in the car so they could leave. Lou continued fighting Trip. The teenager ran back into the house when he heard the police were almost at the scene. Yvette remained outside. Just as we got back to my car, cops converged from both ends of the block, speeding towards the altercation. We ducked down on the floor of my car as to not be seen by the cops. Soraya was in the driver's seat and remained upright. She started the car. Five police cars showed up while we were there.

"We gotta go," Chuck said to us.

Soraya and I didn't answer. He was right though. More than likely if we stayed, the neighbors would have pointed us out to the cops. We slowly drove off as to not bring unnecessary attention to ourselves. Like clockwork, Chuck and I pulled out our cell phones.

"I'll call Bam," I told Chuck.

"Alright, I'll call Roberto," he responded.

We had to find out if they got away.

"Damn it," I said in frustration. "There's no answer. It's going to voicemail." I waited to hear if Chuck got in contact with Roberto before I called Bam again.

"Roberto's not answering either," Chuck told us.

"Shit," I yelled. "Now everything is fucking up."

"Don't get upset," Soraya said to me. "Just call again."

I did and Bam still wasn't answering. I left him a message to call me back as soon as possible. Chuck left a message for Roberto also.

"There's nothing we can do here," Soraya said to us. "If we stay up here, we're going to be pulled over by cops. I know you want to wait and see what happens with Roberto, Bam and Lou but you have to keep in mind that the cops may have caught them. We have to leave now."

It was something that we didn't want to hear, but we knew that she could have been right.

"Fuck!" I yelled in frustration. "Let's go then."

I didn't want to leave but if they were arrested, we could do more for them on the outside. We got on I-95 south wondering what the hell happened and how everything turned out back in Bridgeport.

Chapter 19

The whole drive back to Brooklyn, we kept calling Bam and Roberto's cell phones. We had no success. We got back to the Plaza and we really didn't know what to do. Chuck decided to stay at our apartment for a while. This was just in case we heard anything or heard from anyone. We didn't say much because we were anxious to find out what happened and we were tired.

Chuck and I were starving so we made a couple of turkey and cheese sandwiches. Soraya went into the bedroom and fell out. We could tell because we heard her snoring. She was very tired. I closed the bedroom door as to not keep our neighbors up with her snoring. I sat on the couch to finish my sandwich. Chuck was not joking; he was already finished with his. We sat there watching music videos and crappy late night cable movies. My stomach was full and sleepiness was starting to overtake me. I was doing the 'Dope Fiend Lean'. That's when you're dozing off and your head slowly leans to the front or the side. When it seems like you're about to fall over, you catch yourself and straighten yourself up only to doze off within 10 seconds and repeat the whole process again. Chuck was out cold. His mouth was wide open and he was almost drooling. Finally, I fell asleep also.

The phone rang and startled me out of my sleep. I jumped up to answer it. I glanced at the clock and it was 4:12 a.m.

"Malik," said the voice on the other end of the phone. "We got bagged." It was Roberto telling me he got locked up. He sounded just as tired as we were.

"What happened?" I asked anxiously.

"We got bagged I told you," he said testily.

"No shit," I said sarcastically. "How did ya'll get caught?"

"Where were you?" He asked me with attitude.

"We were there," I replied.

"Then why did we get caught and you're at home?" He asked me.

I was surprised that he was coming at me like that.

"We were there," I repeated. "We saw when ya'll got there. We ran towards ya'll but when we heard the police sirens, we ran back to my car. Just like when ya'll heard it, ya'll tried to get away too. Yvette saw us. We wouldn't leave you hanging."

"I didn't see you," he said.

"I told you we were there!" I exclaimed. "How long have we known each other?"

"A long time," he responded.

"A long fuckin' time," I said. "So how many times have I left ya'll hanging?"

"Never."

"So why would I start now?" I asked. "We didn't and we wouldn't leave ya'll hanging."

"Alright," he responded.

"Now what happened?" I asked again.

"When we heard the cops getting closer, we jumped in our cars to leave," Roberto began. "But Lou kept fighting Trip. Then the cops just swarmed in both directions and it was too late. We got caught. It took about seven cops to break up Lou and Trip. They were going at it. They wanted to kill each other."

"Then what?" I asked.

"After the cops separated them, wait, before that, when the cops were trying to separate them, Yvette was out of control," Roberto explained. She was screaming that Lou broke their car windows and was screaming for the cops to let Trip go because he was protecting his property. When she realized that the cops were going to arrest Trip, she started cursing at the cops. She was asking them why they were arresting Trip and they told her. She was pointing to her car window screaming for them to look at what Lou did. So one of the cops looked at her window, to fill out a report, and he shone his flashlight in the car.

He had a funny look on his face and asked Yvette if Lou put anything in her car. She said that he put a brick in her car. The cop asked her if Lou put anything else in the car and she said just the brick. The cop opened the backdoor to her car and bent down and came out holding a freezer bag full of weed. You should have seen her face. Her mouth dropped. She started copping pleas saying that it wasn't hers and that Lou must have put it there."

"What did Lou say?" I asked.

"He was already in one of the police cars," he answered. "He was trying to kick out the windows in the police car. Once he was in the police car is when he decided he didn't want to be there. The cops restrained his legs after that. The thing is, Lou must have broken Trip's window before he broke Yvette's."

"Yeah, he did," I told him.

"Well," he continued, "when he broke Trip's window, the neighbors must have immediately looked out of their windows and saw him break Yvette's window. They told the cops that they saw Lou throw the brick through Yvette's window but he didn't put anything else in her car."

"What was Yvette doing then?" I asked.

"She was screaming that it wasn't hers and just going crazy," Roberto replied. "The cop wasn't trying to hear it though. They put her in handcuffs after a few cops had to restrain her. She was resisting and fighting them from putting the cuffs on her."

"So it worked," I said to Roberto.

"Yeah, that part did," he answered.

The plan was to put a significant amount of weed in Yvette's car. We involved Lou because we knew he wanted revenge against Trip and Yvette. He got a half-pound of weed and put it in Yvette's car. Lou used to break into and steal cars back in the day. It was no problem for him getting into her car quickly. We had Soraya call 911 and say that she was Yvette. Then she was to report Yvette's car stolen. We knew that the cops would finally find Yvette's car and find the weed. We knew that when the police told Yvette that her car was reported stolen, by her, she would tell them that she didn't report it stolen. The cops would of course ask for her identification and to see the registration for the car. Once they looked in the car, they would see the weed that Lou put in there. From there it would be a domino effect where Yvette would assume that it was Trip's weed and that if came down to it, she wouldn't go to prison for him. She would dime him out to save her ass.

"What happened with that teenager that was there?" I asked.

"He ran back into Trips house and from what I understand, he started flushing weed and blow down the toilet," Roberto replied.

"They caught him?" I asked.

"No," he answered. "He went out one of the back windows and was gone. I overheard some cops talking and that's how I know that he was flushing all that shit down the toilet. He was rushing to get rid of as much drugs as he could before the cops went into the house. In doing that, he left a lot of residue all over. I don't even think that he got rid of all the drugs that was in the house."

"I knew that motherfucka was still hustling," I said to Roberto.

"Yeah," he answered. "You called it."

"Wait a minute," I said. "Why are the cops letting you talk so long on the phone?"

"I really don't know," he answered. "But I'm not knocking it. Honestly, I think it's because they're too busy dealing with Trip, Yvette and the drugs they found in the car and house. It was a substantial amount that they found. They're not too concerned with Bam and me. They're not concerned with Lou too much either.

"How are Bam and Lou?" I asked.

"Bam is cool but Lou is still pissed," Roberto responded. "They put Trip in a different cell than us. They know if they put Lou and Trip in the same cell they would kill each other."

"Have ya'll seen the judge yet?" I asked.

"Not yet," he replied. "We're going to see him in the morning most likely."

"So you don't even know anything about bail?" I asked him.

"I won't know anything until tomorrow," he stated. "Well, we still have the money that we were going to use to pay for the weed," I explained. "But depending on how much the bail is, I doubt we are going to have enough money to get all three of ya'll out."

I heard in the background, a cop telling Roberto that his time was up. "I gotta go," he said. Then the phone went dead and he was gone.

"What happened?" Soraya asked me. I explained the whole situation to her and Chuck.

"What's next?" she asked.

"Tomorrow we just have to wait to hear from them," I replied. "There's nothing else we can do."

"I'm going to head home," Chuck told us.

"Alright," I told him. "We'll talk tomorrow. Thanks for everything."

"You got it," he responded. I gave him a pound and closed the door behind him and the long night.

Chapter 20

"That night was crazy," I said to Bam and Chuck. It's been two months since we exacted revenge on Trip and Yvette. We sat on the benches in front of my building, enjoying a 65-degree Saturday afternoon. For February, the warm temperature prompted everyone and their mother out of their winter slumber. I'd seen people that day that I hadn't seen all winter. This isn't the first time that we've discussed the Connecticut incident and it probably wouldn't be the last.

"That shit was fun though," Chuck said. "Except when ya'll got arrested."

"You're right about that," Bam agreed.

"Yeah and it's a good thing that ya'll only got charged with a misdemeanor and fined."

"True indeed," Bam replied.

We all could have been arrested that night. Or worse, Trip could have come out of the house blasting. And honestly, if Lou hadn't decided to pursue his own agenda for revenge by busting out Trip and Yvette's car windows, Bam and Roberto probably wouldn't have been caught.

"Where's Roberto now?" Bam asked.

"I don't know," Chuck answered. "I haven't spoken to him today. He's probably with his girl. I'm about to go see my girl in a few."

"Is that the one from Flatbush?" Bam asked.

"Yeah, that's her."

"She's a cutie," Bam said.

"I know this," Chuck replied with a silly grin on his face.

"What happened to that other girl you were seeing?" Bam asked. "Her name is Tina, right?

"Yeah, Tina," Chuck answered. "She's been gone. Where have you been?"

"I can't keep track of all your women," Bam said.

Bam's attention was diverted to the street. "Look it's Yvette," he said. We all looked and sure enough, it was her. She was driving by herself, slowly. The strange thing was that she was looking dead at us. It was more of a glare actually. She finally broke her stare and continued driving down the block.

"If looks could kill, you'd be dead, Malik," Chuck joked.

"Yeah, she hates you," Bam added.

"She wasn't looking at me," I said. "She was looking at you Chuck."

"Hell no!" Chuck proclaimed. "I think she was looking at Bam."

We all laughed. We can laugh now. After the Bridgeport incident, Roberto, Bam, Lou, Trip and Yvette were arrested. Bam and Roberto were charged with assault. Even though they told police that they were only trying to break up the fight between Lou and Trip, the neighbors who witnessed it, said otherwise. Bam and Roberto spent the night in jail and pleaded guilty to assault. They paid a fine and were out. Lou on the other hand, had numerous charges against him: breaking Yvette's car window, getting caught fighting, and resisting arrest was bad enough. When it was found out that he was still on parole for a gun possession charge and he had a warrant for his arrest for failing to see his parole officer, it got worse, back to jail worse. He had to finish his original sentence plus more time for his recent charges. He'll be locked down for a while. He's lucky that he never got charged for shooting Ray.

We all suspected it was him who shot up Drugs' Navigator. Ray survived. He never told anyone who did it to him but the streets pretty much knew that Lou did it. The streets don't lie. The only reason he didn't shoot Trip when he confronted him was because we stressed him not to bring any weapons. Just in case we got caught. It's a good thing he didn't. Shit would have been much worse. The story with Yvette and Trip is even more interesting.

When cops found the drugs in Yvette's car and Trip's house, they of course got bagged. Trip was selling weed and cocaine. Yvette knew that he was. The way that I understand it is, the District Attorney pretty much knew the weed wasn't hers. They probably thought that she was holding it for him. I don't know. I do know that they didn't want her anyway; they wanted Trip. They made her a deal, evidently, that she couldn't and didn't refuse. Give up everything on Trip or she would be doing a long bid. She chose to keep her ass out of jail. Reluctantly or not, she gave them the names of his associates and suppliers. She also gave them the information on his drug transactions, finances and violent incidents. Some of which included Mack's killing, Rick getting beat down and M.J. being shot. After she was done talking to them, the D.A.'s office decided to hit him with C.C.E. or Continuing Criminal Enterprise charges. One count of which gets you a minimum mandatory imprisonment of 20 years. Put that on top of all his other charges and he's facing life without the possibility of parole. He's fighting the charges in court but it's not looking good for him. Fuck him. I hope he rots.

Yvette is on the streets as is evident by her drive-by staring. I don't see her too much. I was surprised that I saw her today. When I do see her though, it's always dirty looks I get from her.

"Right?" Chuck asked me. I didn't hear his question, as I was deep in thought.

"What?" I asked him so he could repeat his question.

"I know you're happy that the plan worked," he said.

"No question," I responded. "Except for what happened to Bam and Roberto."

"What about Lou?" Chuck asked me.

"Him too," I replied. "But c'mon, if he didn't do that dumb shit of breaking the windows, all of us would have gotten away."

"I know," Bam agreed. "But we got Drugs and Trip and they're the main ones. I know we didn't get those dudes that shot M.J., but we'll get them sooner or later."

"I guess," I answered not totally convinced. "I'm satisfied, I guess. I'm cool."

The reason I wasn't totally satisfied was because as Bam said, we got the main people involved, but we didn't get everyone involved.

A traffic cop pulled up in back of Chuck's car, which had been double parked the whole time we were outside.

"Hold on I'm right here!" He yelled as he got up and ran to his car. As he was talking to the traffic cop, trying to get out of the ticket, I turned to Bam.

"Who are the Knicks playing today?" I asked.

"The Warriors," he answered.

"I don't really want to see that game," I told him.

The traffic cop drove away a few minutes later and Bam loudly asked Chuck, "You got the ticket anyway, didn't you?"

"He said he already started writing it, so he had to finish," he answered.

"That's bullshit!" I countered. "You don't know how to talk to people. You should have talked your way out of that ticket. Next time I'll do the talking for you and get you out of the ticket."

"Whatever," he replied.

He opened his car door to put his ticket inside when the sound of a car quickly accelerating came closer. Cars speed around here all the time so it wasn't a big deal. I looked in that direction just to look. The speeding car eventually got next to Chuck's car just as he was locking his door. The speeding cars' window opened and a hand holding a gun emerged. I yelled and stuck my right hand up as if that would prevent what was about to happen. This couldn't be happening again but it was. They squeezed off six shots in succession. Chuck was hit at point blank range. He went down. The car sped off and Bam and I ran towards Chuck.

"Chuck!" I yelled as we got to him. "Chuck," I repeated. There was no movement from him and I knew that he was gone.

Tears streamed down my face as I looked at his lifeless body. I looked at Bam and tears were flowing from his face also. He had a shocked look on his face. He stood a distance away from Chuck. It was like he didn't want to get too close to Chuck. Everything happened quickly. I took Chuck's car keys from his hand. I jumped in his car and said to Bam, "I'm gonna get 'em."

I sped up the block in the direction of the shooters' car. I floored the gas pedal. At the end of the block, I screeched to a halt. I looked to both my left and right hoping that they didn't get away. I wasn't sure which way they had gone so I made a left. I hoped that I'd made the correct decision. I sped up the block and I swore that I could see the car about 20 feet ahead of me. I swerved in and out of traffic to get closer. It was the shooter's car at a stoplight. They noticed me. They turned their car into the bus lane and made a right onto a one-way street. I swerved to the extreme right, into the bus lane, and made a right also. Both cars drove towards oncoming traffic. The shooters' car would swerve to avoid an approaching car and I would swerve to avoid a head-on collision also. The oncoming cars were furiously beeping their horn at both cars. I was beeping my horns as well.

The shooters' car was coming to an intersection. At that intersection, they were about to make a left turn. There was a UPS truck coming towards them and they tried to make the left before the UPS got close. They misjudged the distance and speed of the truck because as they started to make the turn, the UPS truck crashed into the back of the shooters' car. This caused the car to spin numerous times only to be stopped by the streetlight pole it crashed into. I safely made the left turn and jumped out of the car.

I ran towards the mangled mass of metal as a crowd gathered. I wanted to kick the shit out of everyone in that car. As I got closer, all I saw was blood. There was no movement. I walked to the passenger side and was stunned. It was one of the teens that shot M.J. His head was on the headrest with blood pouring out of his mouth. He put his head forward and turned to look at me. He looked like he wanted sympathy or some type of help. Towards him, my heart was cold. I stared at him and quietly mouthed, "I got you motherfucka. I got you."

He leaned his head back on the headrest and I walked to the driver's side. I couldn't see the driver's face. The car was badly damaged and no one could really see the driver. It was that bad. I decided to wait for the ambulance to arrive. I had to see the driver. As I waited, I had a rush of conflicted emotions. I couldn't believe Chuck was gone. They fuckin' killed Chuck. I was glad that I got one of the dudes that shot M.J., but it wasn't satisfying. I grew up and been through a lot of shit with Chuck. Now, he's gone, murdered. All of these thoughts went through my mind until the ambulances and police arrived. In what seem like an eternity, they extracted both bodies from the wreckage. They were both dead. I looked at the driver and while I couldn't be sure, because of the blood and all, it looked like him. It looked like the other teen that shot M.J. Maybe it was just wishful thinking on my part. Maybe it wasn't him. But I decided then and there that it was over. I stared as they were put into body bags and I felt that I had finally gotten my bittersweet revenge.

Chapter 21

It seemed like the whole neighborhood was at Chuck's funeral. It was good to see people come out and show their respect for a man who was genuinely a good person. I know when people pass on other people only talk about the good things about them. I'm not saying that he was a perfect person --no one is. He was a good guy though and he was my friend.

I've known him for a long time. Ever since he was ready to fight Ralphie Santoro for saying his breath smelled like hot shit. I broke them up before any punches were thrown. We've been cool ever since. We've been through many wars together. There's been so many that I lost count a long time ago. We've always had each other's back and I could always count on him, no matter what. He would also help people in the neighborhood with whatever he could. If it was within his power to help someone, he would. He helped me with the Drugs and Trip incidents. I couldn't help but feel guilty that my obsession for revenge got him killed. I know I shouldn't beat myself up about that but he was helping me. I feel it was my fault that he is gone. All the planning and preparation couldn't prevent what happened to him. So how smart could've I been to let it happen. We could have just got some guns and shot everyone involved in what happened to M.J. That's not how we wanted to do it. We'd like to think that we're more intelligent than that. We purposely chose not to use the violent route. Instead we manipulated situations to our benefit. That's nothing new. If you go to any business, whether it's a small company or large corporation, people manipulate situations every day. That's what we chose to do.

All of this bullshit started because of Mack and Lou's disrespect of Yvette. Because they disrespected a woman, it started a domino effect of events. This brings us to where we are right now, standing at the cemetery, burying my friend. I ask myself, "Was it worth it?" Was everything we had done really worth it? Did the ends justify the means? That's a question that I can't answer objectively at this time. All I do know is that my family and friends are healthy and the people responsible for M.J. being shot are in jail or dead. I also know and will never forget that my friend, Chuck, will never be back. I will miss him.

I hope you continue to look out for me from above and always know that I'll never forget you.

ORDER FORM
Triple Crown Publications
PO Box 247378
Columbus, OH 43224
1-800-Book-Log

NAME	
ADDRESS	
CITY	
STATE	
ZIP	

TITLES	PRICE
A Hood Legend	$15.00
A Hustler's Son	$15.00
A Hustler's Wife	$15.00
A Project Chick	$15.00
Always A Queen	$15.00
Amongst Thieves	$15.00
Betrayed	$15.00
Bitch	$15.00
Bitch Reloaded	$15.00
Black	$15.00
Black and Ugly	$15.00
Blinded	$15.00
Buffie the Body 2009 Calendar	$20.00
Cash Money	$15.00
Chances	$15.00
Chyna Black	$15.00
Contagious	$15.00
Crack Head	$15.00
Cream	$15.00

SHIPPING/HANDLING
1-3 books $5.00
4-9 books $9.00
$1.95 for each add'l book

TOTAL $_____

FORMS OF ACCEPTED PAYMENTS:
Postage Stamps, Personal or Institutional Checks &
Money Orders.
All mail-in orders take 5-7 business days to be delivered.

ORDER FORM
Triple Crown Publications
PO Box 247378
Columbus, OH 43224
1-800-Book-Log

NAME	
ADDRESS	
CITY	
STATE	
ZIP	

TITLES	PRICE
Cut Throat	$15.00
Dangerous	$15.00
Dime Piece	$15.00
Dirty Red *Hardcover	$20.00
Dirty Red *Paperback	$15.00
Dirty South	$15.00
Diva	$15.00
Dollar Bill	$15.00
Down Chick	$15.00
Flipside of The Game	$15.00
For the Strength of You	$15.00
Game Over	$15.00
Gangsta	$15.00
Grimey	$15.00
Grindin' *Hardcover	$10.00
Hold U Down	$15.00
Hoodwinked	$15.00
How to Succeed in the Publishing Game	$20.00
In Cahootz	$15.00
Keisha	$15.00

SHIPPING/HANDLING
1-3 books $5.00
4-9 books $9.00
$1.95 for each add'l book

TOTAL $_____

FORMS OF ACCEPTED PAYMENTS:
Postage Stamps, Personal or Institutional Checks &
Money Orders.
All mail-in orders take 5-7 business days to be
delivered.

ORDER FORM

Triple Crown Publications
PO Box 247378
Columbus, OH 43224
1-800-Book-Log

NAME	
ADDRESS	
CITY	
STATE	
ZIP	

	TITLES	PRICE
	Larceny	$15.00
	Let That Be the Reason	$15.00
	Life	$15.00
	Life's A Bitch	$15.00
	Love & Loyalty	$15.00
	Me & My Boyfriend	$15.00
	Menage's Way	$15.00
	Mina's Joint	$15.00
	Mistress of the Game	$15.00
	Queen	$15.00
	Rage Times Fury	$15.00
	Road Dawgz	$15.00
	Sheisty	$15.00
	Stacy	$15.00
	Still Dirty *Hardcover	$20.00
	Still Sheisty	$15.00
	Street Love	$15.00
	Sunshine & Rain	$15.00
	The Bitch is Back	$15.00

SHIPPING/HANDLING
1-3 books $5.00
4-9 books $9.00
$1.95 for each add'l book

TOTAL $_____

FORMS OF ACCEPTED PAYMENTS:
Postage Stamps, Personal or Institutional Checks &
Money Orders.
All mail-in orders take 5-7 business days to be delivered.

ORDER FORM
Triple Crown Publications
PO Box 247378
Columbus, OH 43224
1-800-Book-Log

NAME	
ADDRESS	
CITY	
STATE	
ZIP	

TITLES	PRICE
The Game	$15.00
The Hood Rats	$15.00
The Pink Palace	$15.00
The Set Up	$15.00
Torn	$15.00
Whore	$15.00

SHIPPING/HANDLING
1-3 books $5.00
4-9 books $9.00
$1.95 for each add'l book

TOTAL $_____

FORMS OF ACCEPTED PAYMENTS:
Postage Stamps, Institutional Checks & Money
Orders, All mail in orders take 5-7 Business
days to be delivered